PENGUIN
2754
LUDMILA and T

Paul Gallico was born in New York City, of Italian and Austrian parentage, in 1897, and attended Columbia University. From 1922 to 1936 he worked on the New York *Daily News* as sports editor, columnist and assistant managing editor. In 1936 he bought a house on top of a hill at Salcombe in South Devon and settled down for a year with a Great Dane and twenty-three assorted cats. It was in 1941 that he made his name with *The Snow Goose*, a classic little story of Dunkirk which became a world-wide best-seller and is now available in Penguins. Having served as a gunner's mate in the U.S. Navy in 1918, he was again active as a war correspondent with the American Expeditionary Force in 1944. Paul Gallico, who lives in Monaco, is a first-class fencer and a keen sea-fisherman. His books, which have achieved exceptionally high sales on both sides of the Atlantic, include *Jennie* (1950), *Flowers for Mrs Harris* (1958), *Mrs Harris Goes to New York* (1960), *Thomasina* (1957), *Love of Seven Dolls* (1954) and *Trial by Terror* (1952) – all of which are available in Penguins. His *Adventures of Hiram Holliday* is being published in Penguins at the same time as this book. He has also written *The Steadfast Man*, a scholarly study of St Patrick, and *The Hurricane Story* (1959), a 'biography' of the famous fighter-plane. His latest books are *Love, Let Me Not Hunger* (1963), *The Hand of Mary Constable* (1964), *Mrs Harris, M.P.* (1965), and *The Man Who Was Magic* (1966).

PAUL GALLICO

Ludmila and *The Lonely*

Countess Pfalz-Fein

PENGUIN BOOKS

Penguin Books Ltd, Harmondsworth, Middlesex, England
Penguin Books Australia Ltd, Ringwood, Victoria, Australia

—

Ludmila first published by Michael Joseph 1955
The Lonely first published by Michael Joseph 1947
Published in one volume in Penguin Books 1967
Copyright © Doubleday & Co. Inc., 1959, 1947

—

Made and printed in Great Britain by
Hazell Watson & Viney Ltd
Aylesbury, Bucks
Set in Linotype Plantin

Ludmila

Drawings by Reisie Lonette

To

Baroness Ludmila von Falz-Fein

PART way up the valley from Steg, in the Principality of Liechtenstein, where the torrent Malbun comes tumbling down its glacial bed from the peaks of the *Ochsenkopf* and *Silberhorn*, you will find the shrine of Saint Ludmila, *Die heilige Notburga*, in a niche cut into the solid rock above the rushing waters.

It is a sweet figure in milkmaid's dress with the golden rays of the sun behind her head in place of the usual halo. In one hand she holds a harvesting sickle, and in the other a milk jug, for she is the patron saint of the dairymen, the herdsmen, milkers, butter separators and cheese-makers, and the taupe-coloured Alpine cattle with the broad heads, curving horns and large, gentle eyes are under her special protection.

Indeed, her connexion with such is plain for all to see since beneath the feet of the figure there is affixed the whitened skull and greyish horns of what must once have been rather a small cow.

The younger generations, no longer brought up as were their fathers on the legends of the mountains, are unaware of its significance, but many of the local patriarchs remember what they learned at their mother's knee of the miracle that happened more than a hundred years ago, performed by the holy Notburga, the sainted milkmaid, the time of the annual return of the cattle at the end of the summer from the high pasturage to Vaduz in the Rhine Valley below.

All those connected with the event are long since dead,

Alois, the bearded, hard-headed, chief herdsman and his brown-haired daughter, Ludmila, who was then only seven, and named after the saint, Father Polda, the mountain priest, chaplain of Steg, and of course the little Weakling, whose skull and horns adorn the shrine of the patron saint of all milch cows.

However, you may still see the gay and colourful ceremony that takes place in Liechtenstein each autumn when the first threat of snow comes to the high passes and the cattle begin to cough in the early gusts of cold wind that sweep down from the *Sareiserjoch* and the glaciers behind the *Wildberg* and *Panülerkopf*.

There is a valley tucked away behind the granite wall of the Three Sisters above Schaan, in Liechtenstein, the *Saminatal*, leading to Malbun, five thousand feet above the meandering Rhine. It is famous for its rich grass and quiet, protected pasturage, where are to be encountered from time to time scattered plants of that herb not found in the lowlands, one of the rare *Garbengewächse*, of the Species *Alchemilla*, which the Liechtensteiners call by the beautiful name of *Mutterkraut* — or 'Mother's weed,' for it is believed to increase the flow of milk, and the herdsmen are invariably on the look-out for the yellow-flowered broad-leafed plants which seem to grow best in those shaded spots where the snow has lain the longest during the winter when the valley is buried under snow and ice.

It is the custom of the peasants in Liechtenstein each spring to send their cattle up into the mountains and through the tunnel cut through a quarter mile of solid rock near Steg that gives access to this hidden, enchanted valley. They go in charge of herdsmen, dairymen and cheese-makers who move up with the beasts taking their families with them in horse-drawn wooden carts.

There they remain for the entire summer, living in the high Alpine huts, tending the cattle at pasturage, milking them, making the rich yellow cheeses and creamy butter on the spot and keeping careful record of the yield of each animal. There is no contact with the valley below. Herds and herdsmen vanish not to reappear until mid-September.

But then, what a day!

The peasants come from miles around to gather at Gnalp, below the Kulm at the mouth of the tunnel. From Triesen, Vaduz, Balzers and Schaan, in the *Rheintal* below, the citizens climb the mountain lining the winding roads, to cheer and wave to the returning wanderers, crowding as close as possible to see which and whose cow will be the first to emerge from the tunnel leading all the rest as signal of her championship.

The *Abfahrt* or descent takes place in the early morning with the sun shining over the *Rheintal*, warming the first nip in the clear mountain air. At first there is only the eager chatter of the citizens as they wait, the cries of children at play and the distant rush of mountain torrents. But then as a deep, hollow booming is heard from the dark recesses of the tunnel, an expectant hush falls upon the waiting throng. It is the sound of the giant bell of copper cast especially for this occasion, and hung around the neck of the leading animal.

Louder and louder grows the clanging, as the herd approaches, stiller and stiller the people until with all the drama of a star actor suddenly bursting upon the stage, the champion of champions emerges into the light and stands for a moment, framed by the dark mouth of the tunnel.

She presents a strange and beautiful sight. Around her soft, fawn-coloured neck suspended from a shining dark leather collar hangs the huge copper bell decorated on all sides with silver hearts and stars and fitted with a silver clapper. This with her position as leader of the procession confirms her as best cow of the high pastures, best cow of the summer, best beast in the land.

On her forehead she wears a crimson heart or cross to indicate her milk or cream has passed the average. But most striking of all, revealing her as first in her herd in yield of milk, butter and cheese, her one-legged milking stool has been affixed to the broad and noble head between the graceful sweep of the horns.

It is tied there upside down like the gay hat of a maid in spring, beribboned with streamers of the red and blue of Liechtenstein, crimson and white, silver and gold. A wreath fashioned of laurel leaves is woven about her head; cockades of red, white and blue are at her ears, bunches of meadow flowers make gay the leather of her collar. One can only gaze at her with astonishment and admiration, for her simple, unobtrusive, natural beauty has been enhanced a hundredfold.

The procession winds out of the long tunnel and down the mountainside, the champions, the next best, the winners in minor classes, each with heart or cross, or milking stool bound upside down between their horns, then the horses garlanded and bedecked, drawing the family carts, the herdsmen and dairymen wearing rosettes of coloured ribbon on their shirts and crimson and azure cockades in their hats, bearing signs 'All of us are returning.' The signs too are cheered. No accidents, no illnesses, no deaths. God has been good. Saint Rochus and Saint Ludmila, the holy Notburga have watched over them and kept them from harm. Another year has passed. In the flower-garlanded carts the fat tubs of butter and the cheeses piled high like red and yellow cannon-balls denote prosperity and the wealth that the Creator, through nature, has seen fit to bestow upon his children.

And last of all, seemingly shamefaced, sad-eyed as though they knew that they had failed, without insignia, or touch of colour at horns or flank, unattended except for the work dogs, yapping at their heels, and the herdsman's apprentice bringing up the rear, come those animals of more common breed or less energy, who have failed to distinguish themselves in the production of milk, or the percentage of butter fat in their cream, or good solid proteins in the cannon-ball cheeses. From their unhappy expressions you would almost swear they knew they were inferior.

By the time they emerge from the tunnel there is no one left to greet them, or even notice them; the crowds had gone off down the mountain accompanying the colourful cavalcade of the successful beasts, leaving the others to bring up the rear as best they may.

It is a day of excitement, rejoicing and felicitation, with the owners of the winners crowding the cafés and opening bottles of red Vaduzer wine to the herdsmen and dairymen. It is a great occasion for the winners.

No longer in the general rejoicing and carousing incident to this harvest ceremony is much thought directed towards the holy Notburga, that fourteenth-century milkmaid and simple serving girl who because of her piety, faith and devotion to the Virgin Mary, became a saint under her given name of Ludmila, devoted to the care of Alpine cattle and their herdsmen.

The skiers returning in the winter at dusk from the slopes of Malbun throw her hardly a glance, and the Ave that once used to be sung to her nightly by the herdsmen is now locked between the covers of a book instead of in the hearts of the people.

It was different in the old days before belief in miracles, magic and all the magical creatures that once inhabited the glens, ravines and dark forests, went from the mountains. Nature spoke more vividly to the people than it does today.

In those times there were still witches, elves, kobolds and little hairy wild men, good and evil fairies and saints that took on human guise and came down from Heaven to assist the pious or punish the wicked. Werewolves roamed the slopes and the scaly dragon with poisonous breath and deadly sting inhabited the rocky caverns. Even the great eagles perched on lofty crags, peering down in search of the whistling marmots were regarded with superstition.

It was just at the end of this period and the beginning of modern times, so say the old men who remember this bit as told by their mothers, or that version handed down in an old mountain song, along with some yellowed sheets of notes left by Father Polda in the tiny chapel at Steg, that the strange affair of the little weakling cow who was deemed good for nothing took place.

Perhaps it was not exactly as I am about to recount, for more than a century has gone by since these events happened, and the skull of the Weakling, as she was known, has weathered snow white at the feet of Saint Ludmila where she stands benignly smiling in her niche. But the last time I visited her shrine I made my peace with her and asked in advance to be forgiven if I err. The expression carved on her countenance seemed to me tender and reassuring as though she knew that I too love these gentle and generous animals and have tried to do my best by one of them.

*

It was in the late summer of the year 1823; the herds were still pasturing in the *Malbun* and *Saminatals*, but the nights were already growing cool so that their days amidst the rich Alpine grass were numbered and the time of their annual descent into the *Rheintal* was not far off.

The setting sun had turned the blue sky a brilliant orange, then soft pink merging to pearl; the plum velvet of night had come out of the east, spangled with stars. The cattle were stamping and lowing softly in the stables near by, the milking done and the herdsmen and dairymen gathered about the fire which the crisp air made welcome.

Father Polda had walked up, as was his nightly custom, from his little chapel in Steg, to sit and talk with the men and their families, for it was mostly under the sun and the stars that he preached, or sought the God that he served.

Alois, the chief herdsman, wrapping his cloak around him arose and awakened the echoes with the mournful cry of the ancient Ave he sent aloft each night:

'O-ho! O-ho! A-ve! Ave Maria!'

From the shadowed figures of the herders and dairymen around the fire arose the words and simple melody of the even-song of the herdsmen:

> 'God, the Father, Creator of Heaven and earth,
> Give us your blessing, Watch o'er our hearth,
> Dearly beloved Mary and your dearly beloved son,
> Let your protecting mantle spread o'er every one,
> St Peter, Thou watchman at Heaven's gate,
> Shield us from savage beasts; in Thy hands our fate.'

The song swelled louder to include all the saints, Theodul, Rochus, Wendelin and Veit, Sebastian and St Cyprian, each of whom had particular duties to protect them from the mani-fold dangers of the mountains, beasts of prey, witches, evil spirits, avalanches of rock and snow, the claws of the bear, the fangs of the wolf, the pounce of the lynx, the poisonous breath and the stinging tail of the dragon.

And of course there was Ludmila, *die heilige Notburga* to whom they sang:

'Sainted Ludmila, milkmaid without blame,
Make flow rich milk in Holy Maria's name,
Fill every udder; speak thy word,
To grace our beasts and bless our herd . . .'

Father Polda smiled in the darkness. None of the saints had been left out. A big, generous man, he was meticulous with regard to the catalogue of the holy, and even though those whose duty it was to deal with witches and dragons might be thought to have been outmoded by the modernity that was coming to the mountains, he was glad they were still included for politeness sake and memory of past favours, if nothing else.

Father Polda was a man of great and simple faith who believed in intercession, the force of prayer, and miracles, as opposed to chief herdsman Alois, who though professing belief, was hard-headed and as might be expected of one who lived out in the open and dealt with kine, practical and unsentimental.

Father Polda said: 'It has been a good summer – the holy Notburga has done her work well –'

Alois grunted in the dark and lit his long curved pipe until the sparks flew. 'There has been plenty of rain which has made the pasturage rich and the yield good,' he said. 'It will be better than last year.'

'Thanks be to God and Saint Ludmila who has interceded for us.'

Alois grunted again. 'Saint Ludmila has not been of much help to Johann Vospelt's weakling. Her yield is far below average. He was cheated when he bought that one.'

'Ah,' said Father Polda. 'The little one with the white muzzle and the ribs showing. It is a pity. Johann needs the money. He has not been well. He has a wife and small child. They spent all their savings to buy the cow.'

18

'She is hardly worth taking to pasture', Alois declared. 'She costs more than she can repay. Vospelt would be better off to butcher and sell her. She could not even feed her calf properly. I put it to Schädler's Luzerner champion, who has enough over for a dozen such. There is a beast for you. Butter fat 12 per cent, second yield of cream after the first is skimmed and cheeses that weigh like stones.' He puffed at his pipe a moment and added: 'There is no animal in the herd that can touch her.

She is practically certain to lead the procession for the second year for there is hardly more than a week left.'

Father Polda did not reply at once, but sat hugging his knees under the black cassock, a huge lump of a man crouched by the fireside looking up into the starry sky behind which were all his friends, and reflecting. Finally he said in a voice that was singularly soft and gentle to emerge from such a giant:

'How unhappy the little weakling must be. How miserable and wretched. I shall say a prayer for her.'

Alois turned and stared at the priest over his pipe. 'An animal has no feelings. Pray that Johann Vospelt gets rid of her before she costs him more than she has already.'

But Father Polda was right, and Alois was wrong. The little Weakling was most miserable and unhappy indeed. For she was consumed by the hopeless desire to win the right to have her milking stool bedecked with gaily-coloured ribbons tied to her head at the summer's end.

It is doubtful whether she had dared dream of leading the procession down from the mountainside, wearing the laurel wreath and the big, copper bell, for such was far beyond the capacities of a small, not too well-bred cow.

But that spring, when with the others of the mixed herd owned by the poorer peasants, she had made her slow, toilsome way up the mountain, through the tunnel and into the high pasturage, she was sure that at the very least she could earn a crimson heart or cross for her owner, and what her simple, gentle soul yearned for most dearly was the decoration of the milking stool to wear upon her head.

But the sad truth, as she and the herdsman soon learned, was that she was not very strong and her capacity limited. She was small and thin, and on the whole not to be compared with the huge, sturdy Alpine breeds from whom the milk fairly poured in great, warm, frothy, fragrant streams. Her health was not of the best and there were days when she gave no milk at all.

She was not particularly handsome, lacking the broad head, wide set eyes and long, curling eyelashes that gave the others the look of slightly ageing beauty queens. She was taupe-coloured, but darker and muddier in shade, thin flanked and high legged and different further from the others by her white muzzle which made her look even paler and more delicate.

The Weakling tried very hard to be successful, but to little avail. As the weeks passed, she fell further and further behind in her yield. And the more she strained and fretted, the less she seemed to be able to produce.

She took her work seriously, eating heartily, cropping the long, sweet grass indefatigably; she did not take too much exercise, or go climbing to higher pastures which might have disturbed her digestive processes; instead she lay quietly in the shade on hot afternoons, ruminating upon what it would be like to be crowned with the milking stool and cheered and acclaimed by the people. She chewed her cud carefully; she spent long hours thinking the proper thoughts about mother-hood and the responsibility of producing milk.

But no matter how hard she tried she could not seem to succeed. When the milker came around to her and pegged his one-legged stool into the clay floor of the stable, he would say: 'Ach, it is hardly worth while to bring the pail to you, poor little weakling.' Nevertheless he would milk her out of kindness, for he was a good man, but the result would be no more than a third of a pail, or perhaps even less as the season wore on, with no froth or body to it, but instead a thin, bluish liquid that was deemed fit only to give to the pigs and chickens.

And the little Weakling would often turn her head and eye the slender, hand-turned milking stool, and so great was her yearning that she could almost feel what it would be like to have the seat touch her forehead between her small horns, and hear the rustle of the gaily-coloured ribbons as they bound it there. For hours afterwards, as she stood in her stall, the spot on her brow between the horns would ache with longing for the contact.

The reason that the Weakling so greatly desired the reward of the milking stool was that she was feminine and through no fault of her own had been denied the physique and constitution that would enable her to play the part for which she had been put on earth. She yearned to give lavishly the sweet milk that humans craved for their children and for themselves, she wished to see herself the creator of tubs of creamy butter and round cannon-balls of heavy yellow cheeses that would bring wealth to her owner. And female-like, she desired that adornment on the final day which turned the plainest of cows – which she had the misfortune to be – into the most ravishing creature. Capped with the milking stool, garlanded with paper flowers of all colours, beribboned in maroon and blue, she was sure she would please every eye and would arouse the admiration and appreciation of all.

You who believe that animals are dumb and incapable of reason or emotions similar to those experienced by humans will of course continue to do so. I ask you only to think of the yearning and heartache that is the lot of the poor and not-so-favoured woman, as she stares through the glass of the shop window at a gay Easter hat, a particularly fetching frock, the sheerest of stockings, or a pair of shoes with little bows that seem to dance all by themselves; lovable articles, desirable articles, magic articles out of her reach since she can neither buy them, nor earn them as a gift, yet things that she knows would transform her in a moment from someone drab and unnoticed, into a sparkling queen, a ravishing beauty that would draw all eyes to her. Or, if not all eyes, then at least a few, and if not a few, then just one pair of eyes, and in the end, the only pair that mattered.

How deep and melancholy is the wish to be beautiful and loved, to be lauded and admired, praised and desired. What power there lies behind the yearning within the feminine heart; what mountains have been moved, armies destroyed, thrones toppled, nations devastated, because of that feminine hunger for something bright, such as a ribbon, a bangle, a diamond, a crown, or the glitter in a man's eye. What civilizations have been built and worlds discovered to satisfy her craving for adornment, to confirm her belief that if only her body were outlined in silks from Cathay and her eyes ringed with khol from Ind no man could resist her.

Can you really believe that such gigantic forces are engendered and shared only by humans, that this desire to be noticed and admired has not its counterpart in the animal kingdom?

If but the hundredth part of a woman's yearning from time to time for something beautiful to place upon her head, or at her throat, or in her ears, or on her back was what the little Weakling was experiencing in her desire to be distinguished as the most successful and desirable of her sex, then she was still the most miserable, unhappiest and most forlorn of all cows. For as the summer drew to a close she knew that her chances of succeeding were hopeless and that perhaps never in all her life would she taste that sweetness in the hour of triumph that was to come to her more fortunate companions.

It did not embitter her, however. It only made her sad, and increased the power of her yearning. She continued to see herself longingly, udders distended to aching with rich, creamy milk and hear the welcome sound as it frothed into the pail until it filled to overflowing. And then she would feel the milk stool upon her head.

But by the end of the summer, the little weakling was even more unprepossessing. She was gaunt, ungainly, her gait awkward, her udders slack and all but dry. Only her eyes preserved their luminosity and more than ever were filled with perpetual sadness.

One evening, when the herds had been grazing in the lower Samina valley and were returning to Malbun for the night, Father Polda came forth from his little chapel and joined leathery old Alois, the chief herdsman, for his evening walk, and side by side they marched up the path alongside the mountain torrent, conversing to the peaceful rushing of the water that mingled with the musical jangling and tonkling of the deep-toned bells around the necks of the cattle.

They discussed the forthcoming descent, the bounty of the year, the prices that would be fetched in the market by the season's yield of butter and cheese, which would mean prosperity for all the valley, all except poor farmer Vospelt whose weakling cow had yielded so little.

Thus the subject of the Weakling was revived, and Father Polda noted that they had already passed the shrine of Saint Ludmila in her niche in the rock. He had meant in passing to say another prayer for the little cow, to ask the holy Notburga to intercede not only for the unfortunate animal, but also for farmer Vospelt who needed the money so much for his family. He realized that it was too late for such intercession to do much good unless by a miracle, but he also believed there was no harm in trying.

They heard a sharp barking, and as they looked back they saw that Alois' work dog was yapping at the heels of the poor Weakling who as usual had fallen behind the others in the

24

ascent, and was making no attempt to continue, nor was she paying the slightest attention to the animal baying at her heels.

Instead, as the two men gazed they could see that she had turned broadside to the path and was standing staring across the white-frothed torrent to the figure of Saint Ludmila, or rather the doll-like image of her that had been created by Anton the woodcarver of Steg, many, many years ago.

Since there were no pictures extant of *die heilige Notburga*, the woodcarver had taken the expression he had carved on her face from his own heart, one that had likewise loved the gentle members of the Creator's animal kingdom to whom He had assigned the task of extending the bounty of their motherhood to man.

Thus her smile was warm, tender, loving and yet infinitely pitying too and invited a similar expression to the lips of all those who passed and paused, and many, seeing her, would murmur: 'Dear Saint Ludmila, holy Notburga, give the sweetness and warmth of your protection to me likewise.'

And so the two men saw Saint Ludmila smiling down at the little Weakling, and the Weakling standing there, unmindful of the dog that other times would have terrified her, and gazing up at the holy Notburga, her eyes filled with hopeless and gentle pleading as well as the infinite longing and love that filled her being.

Alois said to Father Polda: 'Your little Weakling has grown impatient, waiting for your prayers.' He laughed good-humouredly. 'It looks as though she has decided to ask Saint Ludmila to intercede for herself. She's gone one ahead of you, Father.'

But Father Polda was not amused, for the Saints and prayer was something he took seriously, and he rebuked Alois angrily for levity verging on blasphemy.

'The Heavenly Father takes all animals both great and small under His shelter,' he said, 'but He did not give them the capacity to pray. That is for us to do for them, else He would have bestowed upon them the power of speech. You should not joke about such matters.'

Alois, who for all of his hard-headedness was a believer and who was also a little afraid of Father Polda, mumbled in his square brown beard that he had not meant to give offence, whistled to his dog and they turned up the mountain path again and soon the little Weakling came trotting after.

But this time it was perhaps Father Polda who was wrong, and the herdsman who could have been right.

For a prayer need not be a rhetorical address, or an itemized petition, or lips moved soundlessly inside a cathedral, or even words spoken into the air. A prayer may be a wordless inner longing, a sudden outpouring of love, a yearning within the

soul to be for a moment united with the infinite and the good, a humbleness that needs no abasement or speech to express, a cry in the darkness for help when all seems lost, a song, a poem, a kind deed, a reaching for beauty, or the strong, quiet inner reaffirmation of faith.

A prayer in fact can be anything that is created of God that turns to God.

The little Weakling did not know that she was praying when she paused on the path, her eyes caught by the bright object shining from the niche in the rock. She was aware of nothing but the sadness in her being and unutterable longing to pour forth her love in the shape of milk and thereafter to satisfy her yearning for the beribboned milking stool to be given her.

There was no way she could express or articulate this hunger, but it was particularly strong that evening as she returned with her udders almost flat. The figure in the rocks caught her gentle eyes. She turned to it in the moment when it seemed as though her unhappiness and shame would overwhelm her and she stood there trembling with the intensity of her desire to be as all the others and know the joys of giving as well as receiving.

And so, in a sense she made a prayer, and having done so, it existed; it was loosed. It was directed at the figure of the one whose love and duty called for her to intercede at the throne; and as with all prayers that arise from the sincere and loving heart, it was both heard and felt, in the far corners of the universe. For whereas evil has no power to extend beyond its own radius, the loving trust of a child, or the whispered confession of a sincere and tender heart can alter the stars in their courses. The gentle plea of a maid, asking for a bit of ribbon or cambric for her hair rings as loudly as the Cardinal's Latin in the outer spaces of time or thought, from whence destiny is directed.

Surely you do not think that God is angry at the desires of

28

his creatures to win affection and appear beautiful and desirable in the eyes of others. For He Himself loves beauty since He created so much of it on the face of the earth in both man and beast. And who but He caused the peasants of Liechtenstein to think of something so gay, innocent and charming as the wreathing of their beasts with laurel and garlands when the year's harvest was garnered, and crowning them with the insignia of their gentle servitude, the milking stool?

It was the next day that Alois decided to take the cattle for the last time up to the highest pasture just below the *Sareiserjoch* where the green slopes are watered by crystal springs that gush from the rocks.

As the herdsmen and dogs marshalled the beasts for the climb, for the pasture lay a thousand feet above them, his eyes fell upon the Weakling, and he found himself torn between a mixture of annoyance as he remembered the reproof of Father Polda, administered the night before, and pity for the animal that was so thin and generally ill-favoured. He genuinely loved the animals that had been entrusted to his care, and watched over them.

As he looked, he thought of the long climb and the poor condition of the beast, as well as the plight of farmer Vospelt should the animal die on the heights and have to be sold for what her hide would bring for leather. And, too, there was the celebration and descent to be thought of, now less than a week away. It would be foolish to take chances, for it was a part of the custom that if during the season there was an accident, or one of the animals died, the ceremony of the milking stools, the ribbons and the gay decorations was dispensed with for that year.

He said to the herdsmen: 'Let her be, the little Weakling. She is not worth taking to the high pasture now. She is out of the running for the prizes, anyway. Let her remain down here where she will be safe.'

And then he called to his youngest daughter, aged seven, who was playing nearby, and who too was named Ludmila after *die heilige Notburga*: 'Ludmila, come here. Look after the little Weakling today and see that she comes to no harm. She is to remain behind. Do not let her stray out of your sight and see that she is back in the stall by sundown.'

And with that the dogs were set to work, the herdsmen cried 'Heuh!' Beasts and herders set off up the mountain.

Little Ludmila had brown legs and arms, a brown face, and brown hair, but her eyes were as blue as the cornflowers and wild delphinium that grew in the mountain meadows. She went at once and put her arms around the little Weakling's neck and laid her cheek next its soft, white muzzle, and then taking hold of the end of her halter marched off with her, with the Weakling following on docilely behind, her bell giving off a musical clang with every other step she took.

Some children would have been upset at having their day's play disturbed by such a peremptory order to take charge of a derelict animal that was not good for much of anything, but Ludmila was pleased, for she had for a long time wished to go into the dark glen at the foot of the *Bettlerjoch* a short distance away to look for elves which she was sure lived there.

She was afraid to go alone, for there might be other things there as well, such as witches, or little hairy wild men with peaked hats and long noses and ears who hid behind rocks with only the tips of their ears and the points of their hats showing, or even perhaps a small dragon.

But with the little cow along as her companion, her bronze bell tonkling loudly to frighten away any evil spirits, and her warm and comforting presence there and the halter to cling to,

Ludmila felt no fear at all, and soon child and beast were lost to sight as they left the little community at Malbun and took the path towards Gritsch and the deep wild glen at the bottom of the *Bettlerjoch*.

The sturdy brown legs took the child over a winding Alpine road that soon plunged into a dark pine forest. Shortly they came to a spot where the path split in two and on the right descended sharply into a dark and rocky ravine where fallen trees were tumbled like jackstraws and the boulders lay strewn about as though flung by a giant hand.

This was the mysterious ravine of the *Bettlerjoch*. Mounting, it grew wilder and more tumultuous until it reached to that mass of granite pillars and monoliths with the curiously human forms, which legend said were the Butter Beggars, those wandering friars who came over the pass known as the *Nenzinger Himmel* through the *Joch* to the high pasturage to beg for butter for the cold winter days to come and in return bestowed their blessings on herdsmen and herds and prayed for them, and who one day were overtaken by a terrible storm and their forms frozen there for ever.

But descending, the terrain grew less wild; there were little patches of grass and meadow with many herbs and wildflowers that seemed to flourish nowhere else.

For a moment, Ludmila hesitated to enter this unfamiliar territory, but the Weakling's bell jangled reassuringly, and when the animal also gave forth a soft 'Moo,' she hesitated no longer, and taking the halter once more in her chubby fist entered the side of the ravine by the right-hand path and descended to the glen below.

The elves were there in the form of splinters of sunlight flashing from the quartz in the granite, or filtering through the greenery, dappling the leaves of the trees, and the child pursued them deeper and deeper into the ravine until they vanished in the darkness of tumbled rock or cave, or dense pines where the sun no longer penetrated.

Soon they came to a kind of glade opening out from the lower part of the glen through a rocky path. Here the land levelled for a space, a rushing brook quietened, as it meandered through this hidden meadow ringed with trees, and rich with sweet-smelling herbs and flowers, yellow blossoms with broad leaves amongst ferns, lichens and algaes, arenarias and saxifrages growing amidst dark grasses.

The little Weakling commenced to feed contentedly shaded by a gigantic oak tree that spread its branches in huge circumference and beneath which amidst a scattering of sweet acorns, the flowering herbs and weeds grew in thick profusion.

Comforted by the sound of the bell about the neck of the Weakling and her eager munching, Ludmila explored the boundaries of what was obviously a magic circle on enchanted ground; watching the long blue shadows of the trout as they sunned themselves in the brook, discovering a grey badger with shining eyes working at the mouth of his hole, startling a young deer, coming upon a whole family of little hamsters feeding on acorns and noting hundreds of tiny green-breasted finches and blue-headed tits flitting through the branches of the trees and peering out from behind the leaves.

And in this manner, with the Weakling feeding placidly, and the child, herself turned into the very kind of woodland and mountain elf she sought, playing in and about the beautiful glen and all its wild things, time passed. The shadows grew longer, the air cooler and the sun began to dip towards the jagged rim of the mountain peaks visible through the trunks of the tall pines, and her instincts told Ludmila that it was time to return home.

But the day had been long, exciting and strenuous, and she was both hungry and thirsty. And since she was a herdsman's daughter, Ludmila knew both where and how to provide herself with food and went directly to the source.

She secured the Weakling's trailing halter and led her to a sapling where she made her fast. Then seating herself at the hind quarters she took one of the soft teats, directed it at her mouth, closed her eyes, and began to milk.

At the touch of the little hands, so different from the rough, strong, horny palms of the herdsmen, it seemed as though a shudder ran through the Weakling. For the first moment as the child tugged, first at one then at another, there was no response. Not even the thin bluish trickle rewarded her efforts. But again, the shudder shook the animal and she stood there, her feet spread apart, trembling as though in the grip of a mountain chill. All her pent-up anguish seemed to find expression in the single cry, half a moo and half a moan that came from her throat and echoed from the pillars that represented the frozen friars of the *Bettlerjoch* above and went sighing off into the peaks. And then her milk began to flow.

A few drops at first, then a trickle, then a stream, and soon, a warm, rich, fragrant jet shot into the mouth of Ludmila, causing her to gurgle and laugh with surprise, pleasure and satisfaction, a sound which surely to the Weakling must have been the most beautiful she had ever heard. At last, she was giving, as God had intended her to do.

The child drank until she could hold no more, and thereafter led the Weakling to the stream to let her refresh herself, and then taking her in tow, set off through the rocky path that led from the enchanted meadow, through the glen and up the ravine on the homeward path. And for the first time since she had matured, the Weakling, her heart filled with joy, felt the ache of plenitude in her udders and the need to be further relieved of the gift she carried there.

That night, when the herdsmen accompanying their proud, sleek cattle returned from the high pasturage by the *Sareiserjoch*, to the huts and stables just below the slopes of Malbun and the milkers took to their metal pails and one-legged milking stools, the miracle of Saint Ludmila, the holy milkmaid Notburga, began.

The Weakling was already standing in her stall, emitting low moos of pleasurable pain, when from force of habit the milker arrived at her side, set stool and pail, seized the nearest teat and squeezed perfunctorily, for he was weary from serving the heavy yielders and was grateful that the day was drawing to a close.

But the first sound of the powerful stream of milk landing with a clang at the bottom of the pail awoke him and caused him to cry out in amazement, as by the light of the lanthorn that hung from the roof of the milking shed he saw the distended skin of the swollen udders bearing such a burden as he had never encountered before in this unfortunate little animal.

He remembered the poor quality of her yield and still by habit, milked on, but when the pail was half-full, his cry arose over the stamping of the hoofs in the shed, the switching of tails and the rush of milk. 'Hola, Alois! Hola there, send for Alois. The Chief Herdsman is to come here at once to see what has happened.'

Alois came and stared likewise, for now the pail was three-quarters filled with creamy liquid topped by foaming bubbles of fatty froth, as rich as any that ever came from the big Swiss champions in the herd.

The pail was filled to overflowing, another was placed beside her, once again the powerful jet of milk clanged against the empty sides, the liquid, warm and pungent began to foam as it climbed up the pail. The other milkers and herders crowded into the shed as word spread of the astonishing thing that was happening to the little Weakling and a moment later there was a movement in the throng and the huge bulk of Father Polda bent over to pass through the door.

He glanced at the full milk pail, the second filling beneath the fingers of the milker, the colour of the fluid and the oily quality of the froth that topped it, and crossed himself.

'Holy Saint Ludmila, Holy Notburga!' he cried. 'It is a miracle!' for he wished it so.

Alois grunted as was his custom when he was about to become hard-headed and did not wish to admit something, especially to the priest. 'Some of these sickly ones come into milk late

37

sometimes. We will see. The milk may be sour, or deficient. Wait until it has been separated.'

At last the udders were emptied, the second pail was nearly filled and taken away to be tested for fat and butter content, darkness fell, supper was eaten and the men gathered about the fire and once again the Mountain Ave rang out – 'O-ho! O-ho! A-ve! Ave Maria!' when the herdsman, whose duty it was to watch by night by the stables, came running into the circle, pale and out of breath:

'Alois! Father Polda! The one with the white muzzle, the little Weakling that was milked last tonight! I heard her complaining and went into the lanthorn to look. Her udders are filled again. She must be milked at once. Come and see if you do not believe me.'

It was true. Scarce three hours had passed, but the milk sacs were again distended and heavy with their burden. A milker was hastily summoned, and again the rich, yellowish liquid thundered into the pail; once more a second receptacle had to be fetched to hold the yield.

Father Polda crossed himself again and cried: 'Holy Saint Ludmila, a miracle, a miracle indeed. Well, Alois, what have you to say now?'

But the Chief Herdsman did not reply. He only stared bewildered at this amazing thing, though it was noted that he crossed himself likewise.

In the meantime, a layer of heavy, yellowish cream, six inches deep, and so thick that one might have stood up a spoon in it without its falling over had gathered at the top of the first two pails that the little Weakling had filled earlier. Here was butter fat and a wealth of it such as had not been seen produced on the high pasturage within living memory.

All through the night and the next day and the next after

that it went on. Replenishing herself, it seemed with no more than copious draughts from buckets of water, the Weakling continued to give of her so long withheld riches every three or four hours wearing out relays of milkmen whose arms became heavy and fingers cramped as they worked to relieve her of her sudden wealth.

Word began to travel of the miracle that was taking place and mountaineers and woodcutters, keepers of hospices and charcoal burners from the neighbouring peaks and valleys came over to the milking shed in Malbun to see for themselves and soon there was no room inside for everyone and so the gentle little creature with the white muzzle, thin flanks and tender eyes was moved out into the open where all could see her and watch the fabulous torrents of milk that poured from her.

She stood there then in a kind of daze, wrapped in the glory of bestowing and the fulfilment of that part of her yearning that had to do with udders filled with life-giving food and drink that now was hers to share.

On the third day, the head dairyman came bustling from the cheese and butter factories next the milking shed in a state of excitement, shouting: 'One more pail, and the little one will win best of her group. She already has heart and cross won and needs only another gallon to catch up and surpass the best of her herd. It does not seem possible.'

It was Father Polda who replied: 'Oh, yes. With a miracle, everything is possible, when there is faith in goodness and belief in the Creator whose will has called forth greater things even than this. She may even, who knows, be the first cow through the tunnel at Steg, bearing the bell and garland of victory –'

But here Alois and his hard head were heard from. 'That cannot be,' he said. 'Schädler's Luzerner has won the right of first cow by many tens of pounds. It will be impossible for the little one to overtake her. For the woodcutter who has just arrived over the *Bettlerjoch* tells me that the first snow has appeared on the *Panülerkopf* and the *Hornspitz*. Tomorrow we return to the valley.'

Father Polda sighed and said nothing, for the word of the Chief Herdsman in all things pertaining to the herds entrusted to his care was law, and no one dared question his commands. But it being Father Polda's first personal miracle, he wished to see it taken to a climax.

At that, the Weakling barely made the final pail that was needed to give her the honour of the milking stool. For the great and miraculous flow seemed at last to come to an end, and it was all that the milkers could do to wring the last drops from her fabulous udders. Yet achieve it she did though the effort left her weak and spent and she was led on tottery legs to the shelter of the stall, fed and watered and allowed to rest for the great event of the descent the following day.

And thus it was that the poor little Weakling whose hopes of realizing her desire to be decorated with the milking stool had seemed so utterly impossible of fulfilment, was led forth the next day, cleaned, washed, brushed, so that thin and emaciated as she was, her dun-coloured hide glistened. Hoofs and horns were polished until they sparkled in the sunlight and at last came the moment when she felt the seat of the milking stool pressed against her head between the horns by rough but kind hands and lashed there with gaily-coloured ribbons.

Streamers were fastened to the stool's leg, paper flowers and cockades attached to her headstall and about her ears; garlands of flowers hung about her neck. Small-boned, and lacking the

41

stalwart maturity of the older animals, her head, graced by the decorations, her sweetness of expression gave her the air of a young girl going to her first ball. She became suddenly innocently beautiful and heart-warmingly radiant.

Now, word of the event that had taken place on the high pasturage had also reached to the village of Vaduz which heard the rumour of how the poor peasant Vospelt's animal that had been last in yield of dairy products had in the final three days, by the intervention of Saint Ludmila, poured forth a miraculous stream of milk.

Outside the tunnel, the crowds gathered to wait in twice the number they ever had before. They came up from Vaduz, the capital, and Schaan and Triesen, Mäls and Balzers, Nendeln and Eschen, to climb the lofty Triesenberg on foot and take up their position of vantage at Gnalp, to see for themselves whether there was any truth in the strange marvel that had been reported from the fastnesses of the high pasturage.

Because it might be an ecclesiastical affair, if true, the Herr Canonicus Josef from the big church in Vaduz was there with lesser members of the clergy in the vicinity, and since if it were actually so it would redound to the eternal credit of Liechtenstein, a member of the ruling family from the *Schloss* below arrived, incognito of course.

Spontaneously, and without invitation, the brass band from Schaanwald appeared, the *Männerchor* from Planken and the girl singers from Mauren and Ruggell. The *Bürgermeister* of Vaduz came in his robes as did the president of the council and the ministers from Switzerland and Austria.

Naturally the attraction was likewise to see which would be the lead cow this year, but behind the huge turnout lay excitement of perhaps witnessing a marvel of some sort. It could of course hardly be true that the poor, sickly little animal they all remembered as belonging to peasant Vospelt, and which few had deemed worth even sending up to the high pasturage, could really have won a prize, much less the decoration of the milking stool, but if there was any truth in the rumours, they were all there and prepared to see.

In Malbun the cavalcade was ready for the descent. Cattle, horses, men, women, children, dogs, all were groomed and dressed in their best and decorated in every manner possible to mark the wonderful occasion.

An hour after sun-up the procession gathered on the meadow near by the little community of huts, sheds and barns where

they had all lived together during the long summer and the doors and windows of which were now boarded up.

Father Polda stood upon a drinking trough and blessed them, as was his custom, and sent up a prayer of gratitude to Saint Ludmila for the miracle she had created for them. Then with cries from the herders, the cracking of whips, the barking of dogs and the gay singing of the women and children, they started down the Malbun, next the roaring torrent to Steg.

First in the line, the silver clapper of the great copper bell about her neck booming her approach, came Schädler's great champion Luzerner, winning beast the second year in succession, milk-stool worn proudly as one who was used to such articles borne upon her head. Then came Gruber's Frisian, and Wohlmayr's Zuricher champion in second and third place, followed by several others that had ranked high. Thereafter proudly heading the last division of the mixed herd belonging to many poor peasants tottered the little Weakling with her gay decorations and sweet exalted expression, looking like a mixture of half cocotte, half angel. At her head marched Ludmila, cornflowers the colour of her eyes braided in her brown hair. At her side walked Father Polda.

The three came eventually to the shrine of the holy Notburga by the torrent Malbun, and here they paused and turned to her as though by mutual understanding and consent, the huge man in the black cassock, the brown, barelegged child, and the Weakling. No word was spoken. Ludmila had her arm about the neck of the animal and together they stood by the wooden rail that guarded people from falling into the stream, and looked across the silvery waters to the figure in the niche, the sweet little doll with the tender expression on her carved and painted countenance.

On the child's face was wonder. In the eyes of the Weakling

was deathless love. On the lips of Father Polda was a prayer. There they remained thus for a long time, so long that Chief Herdsman Alois returned to see what was holding up the procession and thus he found them. When her father came up, the child suddenly left the little cow and ran to him, put her arms around his neck and began to cry, causing him to say: 'Now now, Ludmila, what is the matter? Why are you crying?'

'Because of my little cow who is so beautiful. Saint Ludmila, wishes her to lead all the others.'

The Chief Herdsman was much less hard-headed when it came to his daughter and he smiled at her and said: 'She does, does she? And how would you know this?'

Ludmila stopped crying and took her father's hand and led him to the rail, looked across to Saint Ludmila and replied: 'Because she spoke to me, and *told me so*. Please, papa, let her be the first.'

Alois looked from his daughter to the Weakling, to Father Polda standing at her side and said harshly: 'What is this nonsense? Have you been putting ideas into the child's head? What does she mean the Saint spoke to her? Did you hear anything?'

Father Polda smiled, and gently shook his head. 'I heard nothing,' he said. 'But sometimes little children can hear things that we cannot.'

For a moment the big, bearded herdsman stood there staring at the statue. Then he picked up the child on his arm and strode away down the path. Man and beast followed.

But at Steg, the last stopping place before they moved down the *Saminatal* and entered the rock tunnel to emerge into the world beyond, Chief Herdsman Alois gave brief sharp orders; two herdsmen came to the rear of the procession and led the little Weakling forward to the head of the line. There, while

many looked aghast and all stared in utter amazement, they took the great black-silver star and heart-studded bell with the polished black leather collar from the leading cow and hung it about her neck. They likewise removed the crown of laurel leaves from the noble brow of the Luzerner champion and draped it about the head of the Weakling, for whom it was too big, and therefore fell slightly askew, giving her an even more coquettish air. In her emaciated state from the great effort she had made, the weight of the big bell was almost more than she could carry. Then the halter lead was put into the hands of Ludmila. The Weakling staggered forward and the two, now at the head of the procession, led the way down the road into the tunnel.

It was wrong, and arbitrary what Alois did, for Schädler's big Luzerner had fairly won the right to lead them all home a second year and one voice from the crowd protested, 'Halloo there, Mr Chief Herdsman, what is going on? Everyone knows that Schädler's animal is the winner.'

But with a terrible frown, Alois cried, 'Quiet! Saint Ludmila herself has commanded that the Weakling lead us home!' And thereafter none dared dispute his decision.

Soon the dense crowds lining both sides of the road on the other side of the tunnel heard the irregular booming of the big cowbell around the neck of the approaching leader. It would ting, then stop, then ring faintly, again louder as it approached, more faintly again, and once it jangled harshly as though the bearer had fallen.

Murmurs and shivers of excitement ran through the crowd. Louder and louder sounded the great bell and steadier now. The moment was at hand.

Out of the mouth of the tunnel stepped a brown elf with cornflowers the colour of her eyes braided through her brown hair, leading a small thin cow with a white muzzle, belled, crowned and garlanded. For a moment they stood blinking in the sunlight. Then a great shout went up from the throng, almost like a hosannah, a cheer and a cry and a greeting and a prayer all in one. Men waved their hats and shouted, women wept and sobbed.

It was true. The miracle had taken place, for there was the evidence before their very eyes. Not only had the poor despised weakling won the right to wear her milk stool, but the champion's laurels and winner's position, the prize of best cow of the year had come to her. Only a Saint could have made this possible.

Then the brass band struck up the national Anthem of Liechtenstein, the *Männerchor* burst into song as did the *Sängerbund* of girls from Mauren and Ruggell, and the women's choir from Triesenberg.

His Highness, the member of the Royal family, dropped his incognito and stepped forward to pin a glittering medal, the Royal Double Eagle First Class to the Weakling's collar and pick up the child Ludmila in his arms and kiss her. Herr Canonicus Josef suddenly knelt in the road, followed by the other members of the clergy, and struck up an 'Allelujia' and the next moment men, women and children in the huge throng of welcomers likewise went to their knees, singing and giving thanks to Him and those on High from whom all miracles and blessings flow.

And so, her greatest desire and dream of glory come to realization, the little Weakling, burdened with the earthly prizes awarded to her by Heavenly dispensation, looked out upon this strange scene, the towering mountains opposite, the blue thread of the Rhine in the valley far below, the people in their Sunday best kneeling in the road, the black-robed priests, the stately figure of His Highness, and her eyes were gentle and swimming, filled with love and happiness, that all this which she had so much desired had in the end happened to her, and that before her final moment she had been privileged to give. For the effort and the strain of the last three days had been too much for her, and with that sure instinct of animals, she knew she was looking upon the sunshine and the kindly people whom it had been her duty to feed for the last time. And she was content.

The big bell boomed again. The sun glittered from the golden medal at her collar. Child and animal started forward again down the mountain followed by the gay and colourful procession of the annual return from the high pasturage.

*

There is not much more to the story. Worn out by her efforts, the little Weakling passed away in the valley before sundown that evening. Yet strangely it did not put a damper on the celebration, or the happiness of the people at having been singled out for the execution of a miracle in their midst. They and the Canonicus saw it quite simply as the logical extension of the miracle whereby having performed it and demonstrated her love and power via the Weakling, Saint Ludmila, the holy Notburga had taken the little animal to her as her reward and she would henceforth graze peacefully and happily in the Heavenly pastures close to the side of her loving friend and patron. And it is for this reason that the skull and horns of the Weakling were bestowed on the shrine of the Saint.

The butter and cheese made from the miraculous milk of the Weakling brought their weight in gold and never again would the poor peasant Vospelt or his family want for anything.

Only one thing more remains to be told.

A week later, Chief Herdsman Alois suddenly appeared at Steg in the Samina valley with the child Ludmila at his side and sought out Father Polda in the tiny chapel.

'Come,' he said to the Priest. 'Come with us.'

They walked, all three in silence up the path again past the shrine in the rocks to which Alois did not so much as vouchsafe a glance now, until they came to the deserted huts and barns on the Malbun slope. Here it was that the little Ludmila at her father's behest took over the leadership, and with the sure orientation of the mountain child, led them up the path to the *Bettlerjoch*. As she had once before, she branched off from the main dark and fearsome ravine downwards towards the glen of the elves, and thence through the rock path to the magic circle in the enchanted meadow peaceful in the morning sun with only the sound of birds in the great oak, the rustling of small animals in the underbrush and the gentle murmur of the stream resting before it resumed its plunge below.

Alois now roved about this meadow, his eyes on the ground; he went to the brook, came back, knelt near the oak tree and examined the ground, arose and went to the opposite side and did the same. And as he searched, his dark, bearded face lit up with satisfaction and at last he came over and faced Father Polda.

'Well,' asked the priest. 'Why have you brought me here? What is it you have discovered?'

'This,' said Alois. 'Look there. Do you recognize that little weed with the yellow flower and the broad leaf?'

Father Polda gazed down at the plant that seemed to be growing in unusual profusion all about them. 'It is the *Alchemilla*,' he replied. 'The *Mutterkraut*.'

'Yes,' said the Herdsman. 'Have you ever seen so much at one time?'

The priest shook his head. 'No. It is most unusual.'

'Ah! Then come here and look. Here under the oak tree, it grows almost solid. But see where it has been cropped, and the hoof marks of an animal. Round and about this tree it has been eaten away –'

'Well –?' said the priest.

Alois threw him a look of triumph. 'It was here that Ludmila

53

came that day with the little Weakling when I refused to take her along to the high pasture. Those are her hoof-marks. The little one in a few hours found and consumed more *Mutterkraut* than most Alpine cattle would in a lifetime. The whole day she grazed upon the *Alchemilla*. In the evening her milk glands violently stimulated, she started to give milk.' He smiled in triumph again and looked the priest in the eye. 'There is your miracle of Saint Ludmila for you. It is explained as I always knew it must be.'

The priest remained silent and his eyes were bent to the ground where the hoof prints of the little Weakling were still plain to be seen as well as the close-to-the-ground cropped ends of many of the *Alchemilla* plants which somehow had flourished in this secluded place.

'Well,' asked the Chief Herdsman, 'what have you to say?'

The priest looked up, but his brow was unclouded and his eyes untroubled and clear. 'Yes,' he said finally. 'You are right. The miracle is indeed explained for all of those for whom the miracles must always be explained lest they be forced to confess that they are not as important as they believe themselves to be.'

Alois said: 'You admit then that now we know why all of a sudden the Weakling gave so much milk and of such high content that in the end it was like giving her heart's blood and strength and it killed her?'

A little smile now played about the lips of the big priest. 'That is correct,' he said. 'Now we know why the little one suddenly gave so much milk. Ah, yes, now we know everything.'

'Eh?' said Alois, suspiciously, struck by something in the tone of the priest. 'What do you mean by everything?'

'Oh,' replied Father Polda, still smiling, 'all the other miracles which you will explain to me – what made you say

54

that day the little Weakling was praying at the shrine of Saint Ludmila, what was it that led you to decide against taking the animal to the high pasturage that day, how you came to entrust her to little Ludmila's care – also of course how the child came to wander here to this deserted glen where no ordinary child would venture alone, and how together they discovered this marvellous patch of *Mutterkraut* – and finally of course the greatest wonder of all, what made you decide in one moment to listen to your child, go against the records and at the last minute name the Weakling champion cow and leader of the descent into the valley, thus setting the final stamp and seal on the miracle in which you do not believe.'

He paused and offered his hand to the child who took it confidingly. 'Come,' he said, 'let us go from here.' He turned to Alois still smiling gently, 'But there will be time for those explanations later –'

He walked slowly hand in hand with Ludmila back the way they had come through the rocky defile. Behind them Alois walked silently, his head bent towards the ground as one in deep thought. . . .

The Lonely

The lonely and the too-young conquerors of space and time, the boys-become-men who have lived between the worlds in the silver ships that sail to war and back through the frosty firmament. They are the children of the sky, the wanderers who cannot find their homes. The lonely are those who have come too close to Heaven and Hell, before their time ...

I

At five minutes to six, Lieutenant Jerry Wright fidgeted at the bar of the officers' club of Gedsborough Airbase, near Kenwoulton, Huntingdon, some ninety miles north of London. He wished the leisurely finger of the clock would reach six, when the meagre supply of Scotch would become available. He felt he needed a drink badly, for the Flight Surgeon had just grounded him and told him to go north to Scotland, for a two weeks' rest furlough.

The long, barnlike room, furnished with chairs and tables, with the bar running the length of one side, was already beginning to fill with pilots, navigators, and bombardiers, and was alive with chatter and laughter, the whir and chunk-chunk of busy slot machines and occasional outcries of: 'Son-of-a . . . She almost hit. . . .'

From the neighbouring game room came the click of ping-pong balls and the shouts from the craps table, making Jerry feel even more lonely. He looked up and read again the sign beneath the bar decoration, the silver-painted hundred-pound fragmentation bomb, suspended from the ceiling – 'When You See Two of These, Check Your Gas Consumption; Four – You're Flying Blind. When You See a Salvo, That's All, Brother, Prepare to Ditch!' He lit a cigarette and thought: 'Nerves, my eye. I'll go nuts away from here.'

Major Lester Harrison, Jerry's idol and commander of his wing, was feeding shillings into a slot machine near the door, his cap suspended miraculously, apparently by one blond tuft of hair at the back of his head, an expression of deep concentration on his face. He was a big man, too handsome, square-jawed, with pale, deep-set flyer's eyes and a close-clipped light moustache. Jerry had not dared to raise one like it, but he tried to copy the major in everything else.

At twenty-three, Jerry Wright was an enchanting adolescent whose most serious contact with life up to that point had occurred in an airplane flying over enemy-held territory.

In this he was the product of his class and his family. His father, Harman Wright, for all his mature years and greying hair, still maintained a juvenile pink-and-whiteness, an athlete's figure, and a sportsman's mind, a legacy of looking at life as a kind of noble game played according to strict rules of conduct and behaviour, handed him by his father and passed along dutifully, with embellishments, to his own son.

The war had caught young Jerry midway in the final period of his formative years at Williams, when his racy athlete's body was in the process of becoming equipped with the mentality to match, and put him on a bigger 'team' than he had ever encountered before.

Physically he was equipped for it – a trim, wiry, black-haired boy as finely bred as a racing colt, sensitive, a born competitor with hair-trigger reactions. With his grey-blue lady-killer eyes deep-set beneath dark, heavy brows, and compact athlete's body confined to the rakish cut of his battle jacket, he looked a man and was still a child and was keenly aware of it. He wished he were older and often tried hard to act older than he was.

He was playing war the way he played football at Westbury High and a year or two at Williams. His Liberator crew was the varsity of varsities, and every day was the 'big game', except that he was not prepared by anything in his previous life or upbringing for the encounters with the bitter and awful realities behind the sport.

The Flight Surgeon thought he detected signs of battle fatigue when he had grounded him, but it was only one of Jerry's encounters with reality, of which he was not even wholly aware, the things that happened to him inside when he saw one of the 'team' come home from the 'game', his middle a mass of red and jellied rags.

As always in the throes of this clash, Jerry felt the need to drink to escape from the repercussions. He was aided too by a natural tendency of upbringing to avoid the contemplation of the immediate realities by the substitution of another. Thus he now waited to drink off his disappointment at being grounded and furloughed to Scotland, which would surely put another month on to his tour of duty before prospective leave. He had but twenty missions left before, if he survived them, he would be sent home. Home – Westbury – his father and mother – his girl.

Only a few days ago he had written her a letter full of careful and elaborate hints that their marriage might soon be taking place. His grounding would throw this schedule out of gear. It had been eighteen months since he had seen Catharine Quentin.

For Jerry, his 'girl' belonged in brackets just as did the 'team' and the 'game'. As always when he thought of her, he fell into the mood that the kids back home in Westbury would have described as 'mooning', the adolescent American woman- or girl-worship that has no basis of reality.

Catharine Quentin was Jerry's first love. They had grown up together. Their parents were old friends and alike in station, outlook, and *mores*. They had been intended for each other from the beginning.

She was a handsome, healthy, loyal girl who had been permitted to grow into but little conception of femininity or herself as a woman. Her upbringing made of her sex a handicap that since it could not be overcome, one learned to live with, athletically as well as otherwise.

To Jerry she combined such perfection of physical beauty, flawlessness of character, uprightness, and unapproachable purity that it was difficult for him to regard her as human even after they had both emerged from the leggy, voice-changing embarrassment of puberty into the adolescent love that finally ended in engagement before he had left for England. Indeed, he hardly did.

She was one of those perfect specimens of American beauty which is frequently the result of wealth and careful social selection, a finely proportioned slender girl, violet-eyed, with rich russet hair framing the kind of features that must be reckoned as beauty.

She had the modern athlete's body and carried her own sweet fragrance of health and cleanly vitality. Too, she was possessed of a clarity of spirit and a purity that concealed her ignorance of herself and the world. She had been bred to type and to escape all of harm or hurt or realities of life that might be avoided, as had been Jerry.

All this made Jerry think of his forthcoming marriage to her with a humbleness verging upon abasement. In his boy's mind she was locked away in a compartment marked: 'Goddess – Sacred. . . .'

Life in the Air Force had abolished Jerry's virginity and had even assisted in reducing some of the prudery instilled in him by his family, upbringing, class, and general education. Even so, Jerry did not realize that he never thought of Catharine as a woman with whom he would some day join his body in union to produce his children, much less blend in passion and in ecstasy.

For here was the supreme achievement of the system that made him – not even when he went down to London with the gang to seek sexual release from tension did she cross his mind. So far was his Catharine removed from this concept that he was not even burdened with a sense of guilt or cheating. Since no love or woman-worship was involved, there was no disloyalty. Loyalty loomed large in Jerry's catalogue of virtues.

The clock now stood at two minutes to six, and the eager and thirsty lined the bar and were making leading remarks at the frosty backs of the bartenders. They were all boys doing men's work, and of them all, Jerry felt his youth the most.

He knew that he was man enough to fly his course under attack or bring home a limping ship, to carry his commission and play his part. But inside he seemed to feel no different from the way he felt at home when he was a high-school football hero, or a freshman star, and then briefly a sophomore at Williams before he had enlisted.

He yearned desperately to grow up, not only to be a man, but to feel like one instead of a kid, something between the dashing, virile, swashbuckling Lester Harrison, over there at the slot machine, and tough Sam Bognano, captain of the Liberator 'My Black Hen', of which Jerry was co-pilot.

Sam came in through the door, looking around for friends. A stocky boy with a flat nose and slightly protruding eyes, he spotted Jerry and called: 'Hi! How'd you make out with the Flight Surgeon? Nothing trivial, I hope.'

Jerry said: 'Keep away from me. I'm a sick man. I've got something awful. Two weeks' rest furlough. I'm supposed to go to Scotland and graze. . . .'

Bognano quickly rubbed the back of his hand against Jerry's

neck. 'Oh, you lucky stiff. Lemme touch you. Maybe it's catching. . . .'

'Lucky, my foot! I'll go screwy. Christ, two weeks nutting around by myself! . . .'

'Yeah' – Bognano said sympathetically – 'that's terrible. Fresh air, plenty of sleep, nothing to worry about. You'd better have some medicine right away.' He turned and waved at Major Harrison and said: 'Hi, Lester, come on over and have a drink.'

The major, without looking up, pulled the plunger of the machine and said in his dry, mocking voice: 'I've got an investment here. Something's goin' to bust soon. . . .'

Precisely at six o'clock, when the two bartenders faced around and said: 'What'll it be, gentlemen?' the major's slot machine whirred and went: 'Chunk, chunk, chunk, CRASH!' and began to cascade shillings.

Somebody yelled: 'Hey, that lucky bastard's hit it again! Jackpot!'

Major Harrison came over and dumped his swag on to the bar between Sam and Jerry without emotion, saying: 'I knew she was hot. I'm buying. Straight Scotch.'

Jerry's moment of envy was not for the pile of silver heaped on the bar, but rather an extension of his admiration for the swashbuckling type of man who could coax jackpots out of one-armed bandits and never turn a hair. The most that Jerry had ever been able to ring up was three bells for the twenty-shilling pay-off. He felt that somehow it had something to do with the kind of a man the major was inside that compelled the machine to disgorge by sheer force of personality. Towards women, gambling, and flying, Harrison displayed an insouciant toughness and careless mastery that Jerry would have given an arm to acquire.

Sam said: 'Be very careful of my friend here. He's in a highly delicate condition. Flight Surgeon has just plastered him with a two weeks' rest furlough.'

The major turned and stared pleasantly. 'The hell you say! God bless operational fatigue! What would we do without it? Going up to Scotland?'

He tossed off a straight Scotch with a jerk of his head, and then set the glass down on the bar with a click and a characteristic sigh.

Jerry said: 'I guess so,' drank off his own Scotch, copying the major's click and sigh. He fell silent because he was embarrassed. It wasn't awe, or even remotely bootlicking to the major's rank that caused this feeling, but rather the certainty that the major must know just how much of a green kid he still was.

Major Harrison said: 'That's wonderful country up there. You're lucky.'

Jerry downed another Scotch straight and tapped the glass on the bar. He said: 'It's going to be damn lonely. What the hell does a guy do off in Scotland by himself? If there was only somebody else from the outfit. . . .'

The major moved some of his pile of shillings towards the bartender and said: 'Keep it flowing,' and then remarked casually to Jerry: 'Why don't you take a girl up with you? Nothing to keep you from being lonely like shacking up with some nice kid. I don't mean picking up with some two-quid bimbo, but get yourself some clean, decent girl. Hell, you must know a dozen of 'em!'

The idea startled Jerry. Not that it had come from Lester Harrison, but because Jerry had so immediately thought of Patches, and it was as though in thinking of her so swiftly he had done her a wrong. And as a kind of anonymous public

67

apology to her, he said: 'It's a stymie. The kind of girl you'd want to have along on a trip like that wouldn't go.'

Patches … Patches, that queer little mouse with the grey eyes that were so softly luminous; Patches, with her plain face and straight brown hair, who could sit quietly and contentedly through long silences and leave a fellow to his own thoughts and yet feeling warmed by her presence. Not the kind of kid you'd ever go for really, or get stuck on, but who'd be wizard to be with on a holiday. She'd keep out of your hair. . . .

The major broke in on his thoughts with a cheerful laugh. 'The hell she wouldn't! She'll go.' He downed his Scotch and grinned at Jerry like an older brother. 'This isn't the U.S.A. Girls aren't as puritanical as they are back home – thank God! – or where would we be? Hell, the whole world's upside down, isn't it? They don't think anything of it.'

Jerry suddenly felt stirred and excited and at the same time ill at ease. He wondered whether Sam Bognano was listening, and was relieved to find he had got into an argument with a lead bombardier over taking them for a second run down Flak Alley over Duisburg.

A holiday in Scotland … hills and lakes and funny inns. And not to be lonely. Somebody at your side to share it. … Patches. Patches had a leave coming up from the WAAF. She had mentioned it the last Saturday night they had been together at the dance at the club. Then, confused and disturbed, he knew that it could never be. Patches was catalogued in his mind as a 'decent', or 'good', girl. His whole background forbade him even to suggest such a thing. How would you say it – how could one? He wouldn't even know how to begin.

The major answered his unspoken questions as though he had divined them, though in reality he was only expanding upon his favourite subject.

'You just ask 'em,' he said. 'Put it up to 'em cold turkey. They're used to it. If they have some other guy, or don't feel like going, they'll tell you so, and no hard feelings. That's what I like about 'em.'

Jerry found himself looking at the table over by the wall underneath the big, framed, blow-up of the burning oil refineries at Münster. He and Patches had been sitting there last Saturday night drinking gin and grapefruit splash after the Scotch gave out, and smiling at each other. They never talked much. They just liked to dance together and sit. The thick, blue-grey uniform of the Women's Auxiliary Air Force made her look even plainer than she was, and yet her inner gentleness and softness managed to come through. She was a wizard dancer and never got on a fellow's nerves. He had sat there with her sipping his nasty-tasting concoction and thinking of Catharine and the dances at the country club back home in the fall, when the autumn smoke smell drifted in from the outside.

It was all right to leave Patches that way with his thoughts, because she seemed to have her own kind of inner life that went on behind her grey eyes and at the corners of her mouth, queer lights and glows that would come and go, and shadows that would pause and drift by like soft clouds across a summer sky. And when he would come to address her, she would return at once, and the curious gravity of her expression would change to light and friendliness. He wondered what would become of that expression, what her face would be like if he put it up to her cold turkey. . . .

'But I'll tell you one thing,' the major was saying earnestly. 'If they go, you want to have an understanding right from the start that there's nothing permanent about it. Get it? Pals while you're together, but when it's over, you give 'em a kiss and a pat on the fanny and that's that. Hell, you don't want to get involved with them! But you won't have to worry if you have an understanding before you start out. Most of 'em are hundred per cent. No tears and no trouble. Boom, it's over! ...'

The major raked up the remainder of his shillings and pocketed them. He said: 'Okay, kid,' and clapped Jerry on the shoulder. 'Have yourself a time. And remember – right from the start – cold turkey.' He turned abruptly and walked away.

Sam Bognano picked up the last words and said: 'Where's there any cold turkey? It's Spam again tonight. What was he talking about?'

Jerry frowned a little and said: 'Nothing. Let's eat.'

That night, lying on his cot in the quarters he and Sam Bognano occupied, Jerry thought of his coming holiday, of home, of Catharine, and of Patches, of his mother and father and the village of Westbury, of what life would be like when the war was over, of what Major Harrison had said, and then of Patches again.

He was in the habit of talking his heart out to Sam Bognano, and night after night the two had exchanged their thoughts and problems and simple philosophies, their fears and doubts, their feelings for their girls and their plans for the future. But somehow Jerry found that he could not speak of the thought that always came uppermost in his mind – to take Patches away with him for his rest leave.

It was the idea that was exciting rather than Patches. She came to mind because she would fit so well. And with a girl as plain and quiet as Patches it wouldn't even be cheating on Catharine. It would be an episode of the war to be forgotten with all the rest of the sights and sounds and fears and sorrows to be left behind when the war was over.

It wasn't as though he wanted to go away with someone who

was glamorous or beautiful or even important – in a way, to rival Catharine. In the moral code he had acquired by osmosis, as it were, back home, this would have been a gross disloyalty. To feel about anyone else as he felt about Catharine Quentin was an utter impossibility. They were promised, and his profound and enormous gratitude to her for loving him acted as a constant check upon his relations with other girls he met.

Their two families, his and hers, lived within a half a block of each other on quiet and exclusive Severn Avenue in Westlake Park, near Westbury, Long Island. They were only children – he and Catharine – and their mothers, Helen Wright and Millicent Quentin, had been girls together in St Louis. When the Quentins had moved east shortly after Catharine was born, it had been Helen who had persuaded them to settle close by.

They were good, honest people, but, above all, they were nice people of the upper middle class, who, if they lived by formula, at least selected one that had the merit of wide acceptance. Jerry had not an iota of snob in him, but still he was aware of a wonderful rightness about his family and the Quentins that was lacking in others. There was a kind of harmony about their houses. It was a part of the formula.

Jerry's father, Harman Wright, was president of the Westbury Farmers Bank and chairman of the Real Estate Board, and at fifty-five looked young enough to be taken for Jerry's older brother. He played fast tennis, low-handicap golf, rode horseback, loved his wife, his son, and his business, and at all times and under all circumstances behaved like a gentleman.

Since Jerry could remember, theirs had been a suburban home of easy-going luxury. Since money was the commodity in which Harman Wright dealt, as well as possessing it from both sides of the family, they were hampered neither by any lack of it nor any necessity for displaying it. Its presence was something taken for granted with no particular merit attached to it. It was a family that had managed to keep its youth and good manners. Helen Wright could always be counted upon to handle the superficial impeccably.

She was a handsome matron who had kept her looks and figure for her husband and son as a part of the formula. She regulated their lives pleasantly. Her social position in the community occupied a good deal of her time, but not to the exclusion of her family. Thus the wheels, and all the wheels within the wheels, of her life appeared to run faultlessly. In her bloodstream were the germs of a minor dynast and geneticist. She believed that if the right people would just always marry the right people, the world must in the end benefit thereby.

The Quentins were much like them. Fred Quentin, Catharine's father, was a member of a law firm handling a good deal of the business of the Long Island Railroad. He was prosperous, and he and Harman Wright had become devoted friends, golf-, bridge-, and hunting-partners. They belonged to the same town and country clubs, shared a shooting-lodge in the Carolinas, thought and voted the same way politically. They worked hard and played hard, but always, as far as could be observed, clean and according to the rules and traditions, which had a meaning for them. They were both chaps who went all out for what they were after, whether it was a client, a deal, a golf match, or a bird. They knew both how to win, and how, if need be, to lose. It was in this atmosphere that Jerry was brought up and by observation and example acquired his patterns of behaviour.

He was well aware of how near to his mother's heart lay his forthcoming marriage to Catharine; it seemed as if he had always been aware of it even though he never had the feeling that they were being unduly thrown together. The close friendship of their parents was manifest to both of them, and yet, oddly enough, it affected neither and did not interfere with the course of their romance or their attraction to each other. And perhaps it was in another sense not at all odd, since the two youngsters likewise followed the formula of rightness.

They grew up normally together, went through the phases of puppy love, then girl-hating and boy-hating, drifted apart, renewed interest, saw each other almost daily, and slowly formed the habits and ties that were to bind them together forever in the same desirable pattern. For in addition to being the clean-cut, handsome, appetizing youngsters they were, each saw in the other a continuation of the security they had enjoyed all their lives, a reflection of the best of their own environment and caste.

But not under any circumstances was Jerry able to think of, or visualize even remotely, such a thing as a little going-away together, a holiday adventure with Catharine even had she been available. In these fantasies she played no part. He was incapable of visualizing her at his side by day or by night on the forthcoming leave in the north country. He had for that matter not even a clear picture of what love between them would be like when they were married, the how and the when of their physical union, and on what level it would be conducted. A mother-goddess figure could yield in grace and pity, could tolerate and bestow, but never share. Something like this went through his mind when he thought of it at all, and even filled him vaguely with apprehension.

But he could think of Patches and be stirred and even entertain the liveliest fantasy of how Patches would look when he awoke and contemplated her sleeping beside him in the morning because . . . He couldn't find the answer to the 'because'. It was strange, because Patches was neither beautiful nor sexy-looking according to Air Force standards. She would never be pinned up over a foodlocker. If it was looks and that thing you were after, you would never give her a second glance.

Jerry had met Patches several months ago at one of the regular Saturday-night dances. She had come over from Kenwoulton with a group of W A A F radar technicians attached to operational headquarters of a Spitfire base not far from the town. Her name was Patrice Graeme. She had been in the W A A F four years. Her father was a commander in the Royal Navy and was at sea. Her mother and grandmother had been killed in the south of England when a flying bomb had wiped out their home.

She was, as Jerry saw her, a quiet, plain girl, small, with a pale, oval face distinguished physically only by the fine texture and colouring of the skin and large greyish eyes reflecting blue, sometimes green-and-hazel, lights, and marked by straight, well-defined brows that were rather too heavy for the proportions of a small nose, the end of which she could wiggle like that of a rabbit, and did when she encountered a thought or an idea she found particularly exciting.

She had straight, light-brown hair, which she wore coiled at the back of her neck so as not to interfere with the Royal Air Force cap perched on the side of her head, and a round firm chin, softened by a gentle and sweetly formed mouth. It was the friendliness and softness of her mouth and the curiously eager expression that lay about it, whether her lips were parted with inner excitement or pressed together in silent thought, that really made Jerry look at her a second time and want to dance with her when she sailed by on the arm of a brother officer.

The expression on her face was as though there was always something delicious and secret that she knew, as though she possessed a limitless storehouse of pleasant memories upon which to draw. And indeed there were many – the secrets of a remembered and cherished childhood – recollections of rose gardens and hedge mazes, of kindly Nannies and adventures in enchanted woods in the springtime, or evenings when the sky reflected gold and rose in a quiet stream, childhood toys, a golliwog, and a calico cat who slept with her, and a live ginger kitten with whom she held endless conversation.

When she was a child and learning to talk she had been unable to say her name, Patrice. It had come out 'Patches', and Patches she had remained. She was by nature warm, sunny, and particularly kind, as people are who have had a lovely childhood. Too, she was full of mischief and suppressed fun, but it stayed suppressed because for so long there had been no release. The bitter war had cast its shadow over her, and she had retired to her inner life, where she could dwell undisturbed.

Jerry liked her silences and her presence because they were soothing. The thing was, with a little mouse like that who wasn't either pretty or popular, you didn't have to try to be entertaining. She was there when you wanted her, and when you didn't, she would retire to her own world and you could even amuse yourself watching the inner lights that would suddenly illuminate her eyes or the odd, surprised little movements at the corners of her mouth. He sometimes felt as though he would like to know what was going on in that mind hidden away beneath the simple, artless features and the straight, soft, brown hair, but he was never sufficiently interested in her to pursue the idea. She helped marvellously to pass the time until he should return home.

They took to meeting outside the airbase sometimes, over in Kenwoulton, where she lived. He could call her up when a mission was scrubbed, and they would go to the local cinema together or sit in a pub and drink beer and watch the dart players. She was someone to talk to about home and Westbury and flying, though he did not mention Catharine, purely because he had been bred as a gentleman.

Or, as indicated before, they could just sit and not talk at all for long periods, and yet when he left her he would feel warmed and refreshed, just as though they had talked. He was not aware that little, quiet inner communications between them had taken place – a glance, a cocking of an eyebrow, just the slightest touch off centre, the whispers of smiles or half-begun expressions that formed about her mouth.

Jerry was also not in the slightest aware that Patches was in love with him and that more and more when they were together she wove her dreams about him, that when she went back in her thoughts to the enchanted woods of her childhood, she met him there, that they went picnicking together on the banks of the gold and silver river – he and she and the ginger cat – and that more and more, whenever she went in her gentle mind to escape from the drab and dreadful realities that beset her, there was Jerry with his black hair and deep-blue eyes and wide smile – Jerry as child, as boy, and Jerry too as man.

Lying awake on his cot in the darkness listening to the sound of Sam Bognano's breathing, Jerry wrestled with his thoughts. He wished to God he had never encountered Lester Harrison at the bar that night, had never thought of going away with Patches. Maybe Sam or Lester could put a deal like that up to a girl cold turkey, but he knew it went against everything he had ever learned. If it were some tramp who was getting her few quid for the night – hell, those girls knew what they were up against. You made the deal and that was all there was to it. But Patches was different. She was a soldier and a friend. Maybe she even came from a fine family, like his own at home.

And suddenly in the darkness he found himself asking what,

76

after all, did he really know about Patches? Maybe it was true what Lester Harrison had said about girls here being different from back home. Maybe he was just being a dumb kid and missing a lot of fun. A guy had to cut that out and grow up some time. Those quiet girls often were just the ones. Maybe Patches had had a lot of fellows.

And he thought then of Patches with other men, and the thought brought renewed desire in him and the determination to ask her next Saturday night when they would be together at the dance. He wondered why he had tortured himself so much with worrying about how she might react, since she didn't mean a damned thing to him one way or another. He did not realize that not until he had cheapened her in his thoughts and placed her a cut above the level of the Piccadilly Commandos in London had he been able to make the decision.

The Saturday-night dance at the officers' club was the usual feverish mixture of noise and heat, sound and colour, high-pitched chatter of English girls, the thumping, squawking band all but drowned in the jumble of laughter, voices, and stomping feet. Pilots, navigators, and bombardiers, shavetails and colonels in their smart battle jackets with their rows of coloured ribbons at the left breast, danced or paraded with blue-clad Wrens, their neat white blouses and black ties setting off their pink cheeks, or husky Land Army girls in green jerseys, girls from the town, fresh from the factories, girls in evening dress, WAAFs in blue-grey, ATSs in khaki – or jostled at the bar in the rush to get at the Scotch before it ran out.

High spirits, high speed, and high pressure ruled the night, for the affair ended at twelve and the boys had to dance fast, drink faster, and love quickly. Already dewy-eyed couples were petting in corners and the dancers on the floor clutched each other more closely, matching the rising tempo of the night. So little time. . . .

Jerry and Patches had danced several dances when in the middle of one he suddenly stopped and said: 'Let's sit and talk, Patches.'

She smiled her fleeting, shadowy smile at him and said: 'Okay, Jerry,' as he had taught her, 'I'd like that. . . .'

They went to their little table for two beneath the picture of the familiar oil works, and Jerry worked his way to the bar and wangled two double Scotches just as the last of the supplies gave out. He returned triumphantly with the two glasses and said: 'This is it, Patches. From here on it's de-icing fluid. Cheers!' and he raised his glass.

Patches said: 'God bless!' and raised hers and took a small sip to make it last longer. She drank because the whisky was a food and helped to heal the aches of physical weariness that was a daily part of living under the war. She wondered what it would be like when she went on leave, to be able to lie abed as long as she wanted, and where she would go. She had an aunt who lived in Norfolk, which was well out of range of the V-bombs, but she remembered, her aunt had made a bad marriage and it was not a happy household. More than anything she craved warmth and tenderness and a few of the little luxuries and amenities of living that had been denied her for so long.

Jerry watched Patches and thought how clean-looking she was, fresh and scrubbed and sexlessly appetizing, with yet an incongruous, coquettish touch of red on her young lips. She probably had the stub of one hoarded lipstick left, and used it only on the nights of the dances or when they had a date together in town.

Now that he was with her again he was aware that there was about her an aura of innocence that made impossible the thoughts he had had of her the night before. For if she was a little nobody, a girl he had met casually through the war, who had helped him to pass the time, yet she was also a person with dignity and some unfathomed inner life of her own, which stood as a barrier between him and the use he wished to make of her.

Major Harrison danced by with a tall red-haired beauty in his arms. Instead of holding her at the waist, his fingers were at the back of her neck, caressing gently, and she was looking up at him through eyes half closed. Over her shoulder, the major dropped a wink at Jerry as though to say: 'You see, there's nothing to it.'

In that moment Jerry would have given everything he possessed or hoped to possess to be like Lester Harrison, to escape from himself into manhood. And yet never had he been more aware of the gap that existed between him and older men.

He drank off half his whisky and set the glass down with the sharp click and sigh, which startled Patches out of her thoughts.

Jerry said to her: 'What were you thinking of, Patches?'

'I was wondering. I'm going off for ten days' leave on Monday. I've wanted it so much, and now that it's come, I'm almost afraid of it.' A look of defiant determination came into her eyes, and she said: 'I shan't go to my aunt's in Norfolk, and that's final.'

Her own sudden vehemence surprised her, and she added: 'Oh, I didn't mean to say it just that way, but I've made up my mind. She's a disappointed woman who quarrels with her husband.'

Jerry said: 'I just found out I'm going on leave too. I've been grounded by the Flight Surgeon.'

Patches gave a little, soft cry: 'Oh, Jerry!' and involuntarily placed her small hand on his arm. 'It isn't anything serious . . .? You haven't been hurt, have you?'

Jerry grinned and said: 'Oh sure! Look – I'm a nervous wreck,' and he picked up his glass, his hand shaking with mock nerves.

Patches smiled with relief and said: 'Isn't it silly?' but her eyes remained on him, searching and harbouring little shadows of alarm. Jerry felt the warmth and concern in them and the friendly sympathy that flowed from her. And the determination to speak what was on his mind came suddenly from a genuine desire to be with her in the coming days, to have her with him, rather than his consideration of it as a romantic adventure.

He turned to her and said earnestly: 'Patches. ...'

'Yes, Jerry?'

'Don't you think ... I mean isn't it funny that we should both get leave at the same time?'

Patches' eyes were on him questioningly. 'I suppose so, Jerry. I hadn't thought of it.' But she was thinking of it then, at once, and her eyes dropped from his, and the thoughts stirred her so that she did not dare to look at him because she loved him so dearly.

He said, fumbling, but carried onward by his sincerity: 'I mean it's almost as though it had happened on purpose – you not knowing where to go, and me being grounded and given rest leave.'

She did not move or look up. Only her fingers stirred restlessly about her glass. She kept her eyes hidden.

'Patches. ... Why couldn't we go off together? Wouldn't it be sort of swell if we could go away and see places with one another?'

Patches lifted her eyes to him, and there was a kind of a trembling at her lips. 'Together, Jerry?'

He took courage from the gentleness of her expression and the clear sincerity of her gaze. There was no anger or outrage in her face, and far back in his mind he heard an echo of what Lester Harrison had said. He continued.

'We could go up to Scotland and sort of knock around. I've always wanted to see Scotland. Maybe pick up a couple of bikes and just ride around together.'

There was as yet no hurt in Patches, but only a kind of yearning to be loved by Jerry, to realize the dreams that had been with her ever since she had known him, to make come true this companionship that had lived so vividly within her. She was but faintly aware of the shadow that lay across her thoughts. He had not said that he cared for her.

Jerry reached over and took her hand and leaned his dark head close to hers, so that she could smell the clean youth and freshness of him. He said: 'Don't you want to, Patches? Gee, we could have a swell time together – nothing to worry about, go anywhere we liked.'

She held his hand tightly, looking down now so that he would not see what was in her eyes, and whispered so that he hardly heard her under the crash of the music and the rising babel of the crowd: 'That's what I'm afraid of, Jerry. I do want to.'

It was as though a great light went up in him. He had not dreamed that success could be so near. It was like coming home through hell with a ship full of holes and an engine shot away and you never thought you'd make it, and then all of a sudden there was the coast of England and you knew if you could just hold her up a little longer you'd see the familiar pattern of the aerodrome below, just one more effort and you'd be home. ...

He said: 'Why don't we, Patches? What's to stop us? Would you?'

She was no longer afraid to look at him, to see the eagerness and pleading in his face, no longer afraid to look within herself.

He was asking for ten days of her life, ten days of a lifetime that she would have given him devotedly. Patches had ceased to think. She had no plan, no scheme to tie him to her with her love; she neither thought nor saw beyond the immediate beauty of being with him by day and night. She whispered: 'All right, Jerry. I will.'

Home was the crippled ship, safe and secure. He breathed a sigh of relief and felt enormously grateful to Patches that she had made it so easy. It had happened almost the way Major Harrison had said – cold turkey.

Looking into Patches' eyes, he saw that they were swimming with tears, and they made him wonder. He guessed that maybe girls always cried at a moment like that, even if they were used to it, and his own sensitivity told him that Patches was not hardened. He might be the first with whom she had ever gone away. And he thought of Lester Harrison again and of Catharine, and he wished that he could blot both thoughts from his mind; for he knew what he must now do, and he did not wish to do it.

It went against the grain, against everything he was and felt and had lived by in the past. And yet he was aware of the essential truth of the warning Major Harrison had given him, and likewise his conscience urged the need of demonstration of loyalty to Catharine. It was as though by hurting Patches he could ease his guilt for a deed about which Catharine would never know, but that might in the future rise up to haunt him. That ghost must now be laid while there was yet time, when he and Patches were still upon no more than the outer threshold of their adventure together.

Jerry tried to think how Lester would say it. He even pictured the major sitting in his place, aggressively self-confident, swaggering a little, completely sure of himself and his attrac-

entwined and holding hard while *The Star-Spangled Banner*
and *God Save the King* were played.

When it was over, he raised his glass with the remainder of
the Scotch in it and she lifted hers too. He said: 'To Scotland
... and us ...' and she replied: 'God bless. ...'

Patches thought her heart would break.

Jerry thumbed a jeep ride in to Kenwoulton Monday morning to meet Patches. They were picking up the London train to
Birmingham and the north when it came through at eleven. He
was early for his appointment and wandered the streets of the
ugly, red-brick city looking into shops.

As always, he was startled to find how used he had become
to English ways and the English scene, the tall buses and the
tiny cars, the long lines of tired-looking women queued up at
butcher and fishmonger with their net or paper market-bags,
the distinctive smell of coal smoke, the homely, friendly pubs
placarding their particular brand of beer or ale, drably-clothed
people endlessly riding past on bicycles, and the characteristic
gaps where houses were missing in the heart of the shopping-
district and where now stood the round, low water tanks as
protection against any future fire blitz.

He thought about his own village of Westbury – the broad
shopping-street with the huge plate-glass windows, the big
shiny cars lined up at the kerb, the quiet tree-shaded side
streets, the kids pouring out of the high school in the afternoon,
the peaceful, lazy games of ball that would be going on on a
summer's day, like this one so far away in Kenwoulton, bright,
warm, and shining. What a day to start this queer trip with an
odd little girl he did not even know very well!

How different everything was from home, almost as though
he were playing a part in a dream, except that he was there

standing at Hadsley Circle carrying his Valpack, his cap pushed to the back of his head, watching a white-cuffed bobby directing the stream of snorting double-decked red buses and military traffic. It might well be that home was the dream.

He looked at his watch. It was time. He picked up his grip and walked the three steps to Bishop's Lane, the narrow, grubby street consisting of low and lightless brick houses where Patches was quartered with her group of WAAFs.

Jerry's heart was beating hard with excitement. He pictured Patches's small, shapeless figure, in her blue-grey uniform and jaunty cap, coming down the stairs, and wondered what he would say to her and how she would behave and whether she would detect how strange and awkward he felt.

He pushed the button beneath her name – 'Sgt P. Graeme, WAAF' – and went in. Immediately he heard her call from above: 'Is that you, Jerry?' and when he answered, she said: 'I'm ready,' and he heard a door close and her feet on the stairs.

And then she came down the dark, grimy staircase carrying a small bag, and Jerry stared and had to look twice to recognize her. She was wearing a tweed skirt and a dark-blue silk blouse, high-heeled shoes, and silk stockings. She had her hair parted in the centre and coiled about her ears, and perched atop her head was a silly little hat made out of straw and artificial cornflowers.

Jerry exclaimed: 'Patches! You're in civvies! You look wizard!'

'Do you like me? I hoped you would. Oh, Jerry, it's so wonderful to wear clothes again.'

'Patches – I didn't expect . . . I mean I'd forgotten you didn't have to wear your uniform.'

It wasn't that it changed the contours of her queer little face or even made her pretty, but she had become a girl, something he had never been conscious of before. Robbed of the bulky stiffness of her uniform, her figure was young and slender; the gentle lift of her breasts showed beneath the silk of her blouse. Her legs moved with a new kind of freedom and rhythm; there was a pathetic slimness to her shoulders and a charm to the proportions of her head and the youth of the soft column of her neck.

Jerry set down his bag and leaned over almost shyly and kissed her cheek. She lifted her hand to his face and held it there, and then they stood for a moment in the gloomy hall of the lodging-house looking at one another.

In her mind Patches closed a door softly and paused with her hand upon the door of another. There was nothing left of sadness or hurt or struggle within her. All that had had to be faced she had fought with alone in the hours of the night past. Nothing was left but understanding love and generosity and the young, sweet hunger of her being.

She looked down at Jerry's wrist watch and said, as though she were reading from a page: 'It began at thirty-one minutes past ten hours, the morning of June 18, in the year 1945 . . .'

Jerry finished: '. . . when he took her in his arms, kissed her, and said: "All clear, baby – let's go!"'

Arm in arm, they went out into the street.

They came to their first rest, the second night out, in a huge, grimy, smoke-blackened hotel over the railroad station in Glasgow, where they secured the only remaining room, a gloomy, high-ceilinged chamber in which the sad light from one begrimed window fell athwart the ugly maple washstand with bowl and pitcher.

The height of the room, the huge bolstered bed big enough for four, the enormous wardrobe, made them feel overwhelmed like Lilliputians. The grey smudge of light that came from the drizzle without was depressing, but by this time they were both so exhausted it did not matter. Jerry was glad they had found some place where Patches could sleep. . . .

The maid who pottered about the room, trying with a touch here and a whisk there to bring it a little cheer, said: ' 'Tis no much for luiks, but 'tis quiet, and I ha' nae doot ye'll rest well.'

The trip north had been a kind of half nightmare of over-crowded railway carriages, dirt, and bad food, and wearied even their young physiques; but it never strained their tempers or altered the patience of good humour of Jerry or the sweetness and mood of play and mischief that had come over Patches from the moment they had closed behind them the door of the house in Bishop's Lane back in Kenwoulton.

They had made the wretched journey, hand in hand, half in laughter, half, at times, in mock despair at ever getting any-where, occupying eight inches of seat together in some filthy, third-class compartment, jammed to suffocation with squalling children, weary soldiers, and nerve-racked civilians, or standing up cramped and crowded in the packed train corridors when they could not get even a place to sit.

Patches and Jerry trudged blacked-out Birmingham looking fruitlessly for a place to stay overnight, and returned despairing to the dark cavern of the railway station, a gloomy vault of steel and glass filled with steam and smoke and clangour and the endless shuffling feet of thousands of half-seen people, wan-dering like the lost souls at the approaches to hell, where dim yellow lights would pick up the badges of the regiments of England, or momentarily illumine G.I. or sailor, men and women of the Army and Navy, or drab families lugging heavy boxes and worn suitcases – the endless traffic of wartime England.

There Jerry had had a sudden inspiration, and, inventing a general and a mission, he chivvied a fusty, wing-collared old clerk in the booking-office into parting with two tickets on the Glasgow sleeper, while Patches stood by in open-mouthed admiration at the beautiful lies Jerry was telling.

When the train came they discovered that their tickets called for two bare shelves out of four in a third-class cabin complete with one piece of sheetless ticking, a thin blanket, and a bare pillow the size of a book and the same consistency. Also the compartment had two other occupants: a gabby little bagman from Glasgow, with a suitcase of apples and tomatoes that he insisted upon sharing with them, and a fat minor official of the Ministry of Information, who lay precariously upon his shelf and snored to wake the dead.

Patches maintained that it was the booking-clerk's revenge upon Jerry for the outrageous stories he had told, and dissuaded Jerry from getting off the train and having his life. The M.o.I. man woke up and informed Jerry he was lucky to get the space at all, and that they always booked four people into a third-class sleeper, and usually everybody got on capitally. Jerry was genuinely shocked, and denounced the system as immoral until Patches fell to giggling again and caught his eye, and he blushed and put her to bed on the lower shelf with his blouse under her head and climbed on to the upper himself.

He lay there in the darkness, listening to the clanking of the train, the occasional anguished shriek of the locomotive, and the incredible snoring of the M.o.I. official. It was a dreadful journey, for neither closed an eye, and the train pulled into Glasgow six hours late.

And so they came to spend their first night alone together in the tall, bare bedroom of the grimy, awful railway hotel. Because they were in the toils of exhaustion when they reached

89

the shabby room, there was no embarrassment between them at the loss of their privacy and the sudden exposure to each other, for of course the room had no bath attached, but only a cracked washstand in an alcove at one end.

Somehow they managed, even though they were awkward and heavy-handed with the need for sleep, but concerned only with seeking the warmth and the depths of the great, heavy, bolstered double bed, which at least looked as though it might yield a little comfort and rest.

When Patches came to Jerry she was in a nightdress of washed-out flannel, and somehow she had managed to weave her hair into two dun-coloured braids. She smelled of hotel soap and mouthwash and freshly ironed cloth – and young girl.

At once, and with the simplicity born of her nature and the fatigue of the trip, she came close to him and pillowed her head on his breast with a sigh and a little, tired whimper. A moment later she relaxed her limbs, and her regular breathing told Jerry that she was asleep. He was hardly awake himself.

The pungent odour of soft-coal smoke, pressed to earth by rain, filled the chamber, and the damp drizzly night was loud with the chuffing and snorting of switch engines from the near-by railway, the thunder and crash of shunting wagons, and the high, wailing shrieks of locomotive whistles. Jerry was sure he heard none of it, but he was to find later that never again would he be able to sniff the characteristic odour of train sheds or hear the clattering of couplings and the nostalgic wailing of engines in the night without thinking of Patches.

They went from Balloch to Inversnaid up Loch Lomond by paddle-steamer, with their bicycles aboard.

Here, on the broad, deep-blue surface of the lake, dotted with green islands, there was no war. There was not even an airplane anywhere overhead, and the graceful peak of Ben Lomond, freed from its usual mantle of mist, lifted to the summer sun and with its bold sweep seemed to raise their spirits up with it to the sky.

The past was overwhelmed by the clear beauty of the scene, the sunlight sparkling on the lake and shining from the green-and-purple hills, the clean, sweet air. Places from which they had come, things that had happened to them, had no existence. This was the world, serene and lovely, and they its sole inhabitants.

They stood at the railing, drinking in the air and the beauty, and Jerry raised up his arms and said: 'God! I want to holler!'

'We'd better!' said Patches. 'One – two – three . . .' and they hollered, until the other passengers on the boat turned and stared at them, and three RAF kids came over and said: 'I say, that's jolly good. Do you mind if we join you?' and they all shouted together.

There was a piper aboard, and he played Highland music that Jerry found wonderfully exciting and that brought a new kind of gleam to Patches' eyes and a straightening of her little back. They lunched for two and six on cold ham and boiled potatoes and some cheese, and drank two bottles of the warm, bitter ale, the flavour of which had somehow come to mean 'England' to Jerry.

At Inversnaid the country had grown wild and wooded, and the queer dots they had seen on the hillsides from the boat turned out to be sheep with long, silky white coats and coal-black faces. Just before the steamer docked they passed a waterfall creaming over black rocks splitting a green glen, and Patches hugged Jerry's arm and said: 'Oh, Jerry, tomorrow, may we go there and just sit together and listen?'

They were given a room together in the hotel overlooking Loch Lomond after Jerry had signed the register: 'Lieutenant and Mrs Gerald Wright,' while Patches wandered away and examined the stuffed salmon and deer head on the walls so as not to feel the little pang of hurt that would come when she saw him write it. She would admit not the least shadow of pain to spoil the beauty of being with Jerry.

The next morning the change had taken place in them. They breakfasted in their room and then dressed and went out to seek the falls they had seen from the boat the day before.

Neither spoke very much, but they were no longer apart in their silences. They stayed now with their fingers intertwined, or with Patches leaning her body close to Jerry to feel the comfort of the touch of his limbs, or sometimes rubbing her head softly against his shoulder like a kitten, or just leaning it there contentedly as they sat on the rocks at the bottom of the glen, watching the falling water together and listening to the music of its descent. It seemed as though each stream or jet of glistening black water or boiling spume played its individual melody in the harmony of the softly thunderous symphony and mingled with the turmoil and the music in their hearts.

Later in the day they walked north through flowering rhododendron bushes to look for Rob Roy's Cave, a cleft in the mountain with a barely perceptible entrance where the famous outlaw was supposed to have concealed himself from the English.

The entrance was carpeted with moss and tiny rock flowers, and there was a humming of bees all about. Jerry said: 'Do you suppose it's really true that he hid in there?'

Patches knelt down and tilted her head sideways to look in. 'Of course he did. Why wouldn't he? Did you know he was a distant, distant kinsman of mine? A long time ago we were

MacGraeme, and the MacGraemes were related to the MacGregors. I'm supposed to have MacGraeme eyes.'

Jerry said: 'Let me see them, Patches,' and knelt too and looked into them. It was cool and dark in the deep glen, and there were depths reflected in Patches's eyes that moved Jerry, and he saw beauties there that he had never seen before. They were together in a country whose mystery and romance stirred him. It was as if a kind of mantle of fantasy had descended upon the slim shoulders of Patches, as though she were cloaked with the mystic antiquity of the long-dead hero to whom she was distant kin and who once might have knelt, tense and harried, on the same wild, green carpet. . . .

He said: 'Why, Patches! They're beautiful,' and leaned over and kissed her.

The next day they pushed their bicycles up the ridge on the old coach road and cycled past ruined castle and turquoise-hued Loch Arklet, their baggage strapped to the rear of their wheels, on to Stronachlachar on Loch Katrine, and from there rode on southwards along the banks of the wild lake and the dark, firred clump known as Ellen's Isle, where once lived the 'Lady of the Lake,' rising mysteriously from its surface, and thence onward to the paradise of the Trossachs.

Their way led them from bare, rugged uplands covered with purple heather and thistle to valleys where steep basalt cliffs alternated with bright-green woods of birch and oak. It was in the uplands that they turned a corner and came face to face with their first wild Highland cattle, great, noble steers with huge, spreading horns, six feet from tip to tip, and proud eyes, their fierceness tempered by a silly set of bangs that came down over their forehead and made them look like movie stars.

Patches said: 'Why, it's Greta Garbo,' but Jerry was fascinated with them. He said: 'Those pictures I've seen of those old drinking-horns – so that's where they got them! What a country! I wouldn't have missed this trip for anything. I'll never forget it.'

They rode on with high hearts until, thinking of his lightly-spoken, boyish words, Patches fought against the edges of the shadow again. 'I'll never forget it,' Jerry had said. And in that moment of weakness she knew how deeply she yearned to have him say: 'I'll never forget *you*, Patches,' just to hear him say it, to have had the words spoken so that she could treasure and cherish them in her heart long after he had forgotten her.

They stayed in the beautiful Trossachs Hotel by Loch Achrey, to rest and play and steep themselves in the beauty of the surroundings, and Jerry wheedled a whole bottle of price-less Scotch whisky, to carry with them for emergencies, from the barmaid.

But the next night, with no warning, Jerry fell victim to an attack of the combat flyer's megrims, which made it necessary for him to get drunk, quickly and completely. . . .

This was the black mood of baffling melancholy and sinking despondency that would seize him without warning, laying a gloomy hold upon his young spirit and darkening it beyond endurance.

It had to do with the horrors that lay behind the 'team' and the 'game', neighbouring ships in the flight exploding appal-lingly and spinning earthward trailing flame, smoke, and debris, the sound of the gasping of hurt men, and the void left by friends who failed to come back.

There was too an inescapable pity that welled in the hearts of these boys who were not by nature destroyers. It could be repressed, or temporarily obliterated, by their harassed, adapt-able, tough young minds, but it could not remain stifled forever.

As always, it began with a thought, some memory or association, and then a reliving of some dreadful moment that touched off a powder train of others that followed inevitably, leading to culminating horrors, the contemplation of which he could not bear. He could not fight them off, and he had not yet learned to rationalize or explain them. Hence there was nothing for him to do but get drunk quickly before the ultimate in darkness and despair was reached.

They had been sitting together in a corner of the lounge after dinner, laughing over the attempts of the group of Scotch and English trippers – soldiers on leave in bulky tweeds, with their wives, Naval officers, rich refugees from the bomb-torn south, gnarled-looking natives in rough clothes – to understand an American comedy programme that was being rebroadcast over the radio, when Jerry suddenly tossed off his drink with a queer, nervous jerk and poured out another with a kind of desperate immediacy that struck Patches to the heart. His hand shook when he carried it to his lips.

She saw his eyes and the remote horror that had suddenly come into them so swiftly, and her warm heart reacted at once. She said: 'Jerry – something hurts you. Jerry, what is it?'

He didn't answer her, did not even seem to know her. Patches had never seen him like this before, and yet the urgency of his movement in drinking had struck a chord of understanding within her. They were of the same generation and had known the same battlefield. Whatever it was that tortured him, she knew he needed help, and that quickly.

Silently she filled his glass for him, and when he had emptied it, filled it once more. She continued to do this until Jerry slumped forward, his head on the table. Then with her eyes she picked up two pink-cheeked sailors sitting at the next table. They felt the impulse of her need and got up and came over.

'Anything we can do to 'elp yer, miss?'

'I want to get him upstairs. . . .'

The two sailors, with the air of experts who had done this before, steadied Jerry between them and walked him out of the lounge while the occupants stared but made no comments. They got Jerry up to the room, where one of the sailors remarked: 'Your Yank's 'ad a bit too much, eh, miss?'

Patches replied: 'Haven't we all?'

The two went away and left her alone with Jerry. She undressed him and put him to bed, and then remained sitting through the night, watching over his heavy breathing, holding his hand, and wiping the cold sweat from his forehead. Not until morning, when he relaxed and entered peaceful sleep, did she join him to rest herself.

Later, when they awoke and went out to meet what the new bright day had to offer, neither spoke of the episode. It was as though it had never happened, and Jerry's old ebullience manifested itself in the suggestion that they ride out three miles to the Pass of the Cattle and climb Ben Venue. But Patches thought she felt a new tenderness in Jerry towards her that had not been there before.

It was on their return from Ben Venue, where they had lingered too long, that their little adventure befell them.

It was just a small adventure, when they made a wrong turning and were overtaken by darkness and a bitter Highland storm that came roaring out of the north, drenching, blinding and chilling them.

Soaking and freezing, they floundered along, walking their bicycles in the pitch blackness, until Patches' continued silence alarmed Jerry, and he stopped and reached for her in the darkness, and alarm turned in him to fear. Patches was in trouble.

He felt it from the way she clung to him. Her body, when he took her in his arms, was shaking with chill, and her teeth were chattering so she could not speak to him. She had been heated from the mountain climb and the subsequent ride, and now the light cycling-jacket she had worn over her thin blouse hung in soaked folds about her. Jerry knew it was imperative she be taken some place where it was dry and warm.

Then his eyes saw a weak glimmer of light as of a dying fire flickering through a window, and he made out the shape of a small farm-house cottage.

They felt around to the door, and Jerry pounded on it until a man's voice shouted from within: 'Who's there? Go away...'

Jerry called: 'We're lost. Can you let us in?'

'No, I canna let ye in. We ha' nothing to do wi' strangers. Go aboot yer business.'

Jerry shouted: 'Strangers, hell! We're allies – friends. There's a girl with me who's sick. Does that mean anything to you?'

There was a moment of silence, and a woman's voice was heard. 'Get oop, Jock. Ye no can turn a mon frae th' door who calls ye by the name of friend.'

Candles flickered and the door opened, revealing a cottager, with a ruddy face and suspicious eyes, and a large woman behind him. She said: 'Stand aside, Jock, and let them in. Do ye no see the puir lassie has a chill? Poke up the fire.'

Jerry carried Patches across the threshold and into the kitchen. She was blue with cold and shaking beyond control. Jerry did not even look at the pair. He gave orders. 'Get me a towel of some sort and a blanket.' He stripped the wet clothes from Patches in front of the peat-coal fire, wrapped her in a blanket, and rubbed her hard with the coarse towel the woman gave him.

'Have you got any whisky?'

The man hesitated. 'Aye, I might have a drop. But it's no got the Government stamp on it. . . .'

'To hell with the Government stamp! And I want some hot water.'

He wrapped Patches in more of the woollen blankets they brought him, and fed her hot whisky and water until the shaking stopped and the colour returned to her face.

The farmer said: 'Ye'll best remove yer ain breeks, Yank. Ye're welcome to spend the night by the fire. In the morning I'll put ye on the right track.'

The fire was giving out solid heat now and a flickering yellow light. Jerry made a bed of the blanket on the floor and wrapped himself in another. The farmer and his wife retired. He took the bundle that was Patches in his arms and held her to him. She said: 'Oh, Jerry, you're sweet,' drowsily, and then leaned her head beneath his chin and went to sleep.

Strands of straight, damp hair fell across her face, and he brushed them away gently and thought how beautiful she was. He could not recall when or how the change had taken place, or even that he had ever thought her plain. It was as though her features had come to take on a special meaning and unfold their beauties one by one. They had lost their individual identity as nose, or mouth, or lashes spread against a cheek. The tender sweetness of each had become intimately familiar to him. He had explored them all, experienced their texture, discovering new enchantments of human architecture in the gentle flare of a nostril, the smooth surface of brow or temple, the innocent and touching gallantry of the spot where her head and neck were joined.

There was a kind of eternity to the low, rough room, the glowing fire and the iron kettle suspended over it, with the rain beating on the roof and dripping from the eaves in steady streams that sounded above Patches' quiet breathing. His mind remained encompassed there and with the companion he was holding closely as if to give her of his added warmth. Here a world might well begin and end.

In the morning Patches' youth and constitution, plus the care Jerry had given her, asserted themselves, and she awoke refreshed and with no apparent ill effects from the chill and the wetting.

Thereafter the days slipped by all too quickly, a dreamlike procession of play and laughter alternating with growing passion as they learned the love of each other, and the tenderness and increasing companionship and need resulting therefrom.

It was downhill all the way from the Trossachs into Aberfoyle, and they took it streaming, all-out, brakes off, sharing the whirlwind of their passage and spending the night at the Bailie Nicol Jarvie, famous, they learned from their inscriptions, for the legend of a fat, little, inoffensive English bailie who, while taking his ease there one night, was assaulted by a gigantic Highlander, who threatened his life with drawn claymore. The game little bailie put him to rout by setting fire to his kilt with a red-hot poker drawn from the fireplace.

They sat drinking Mild and Bitter in a secluded corner of the old Bailie's bar, where the last of the sunlight filtered in through old, green bottle-glass set into the wall panels of dark bog oak, its rays picking up the sheen of pewter plate and tankards, chain mail, swords, and pikestaffs. Each in his own way was basking in the warmth and delight of the presence of the other, and knowing to the full the exquisite delight of not being alone, of having the other every moment, by pressure of limb to limb, by a touch of the fingers, a caress of the eye, a quicker

99

breathing, a smile, the fall of a wisp of Patches' hair across Jerry's face.

And if one was living for the moment, and the other was trying to make each moment an eternity, their appreciation and delight that each had in the presence of the other was in no way diminished.

They cycled on to Drymen, where Jerry borrowed a set of golf clubs from the local pro and played the course, with Patches walking at his side spellbound in dutiful awe of his every shot; and this was a new experience for Jerry to be so sincerely admired and frankly hero-worshipped, for now that Patches' love for him had had its outlet, she put no curbs upon her adoration of him.

Thence they rode southward through the gentle, rolling hills of Lennox, and this was a different kind of country, green and more kindly, contrasting with the stern and romantic wildness of the Highlands, and ever their wheels took them at each turn closer to Glasgow and the end of their holiday. For their time was running out, and Patches had to return to duty at Kenwoulton.

As they had planned it in the beginning, so they carried it out. Patches' leave was up before Jerry's rest furlough expired, and she was to return alone while Jerry remained another five days in the north. He was planning to go to Prestwick and look up a school friend and classmate from Westbury, Eagles Wilson, an A T C pilot flying the Atlantic run with couriers.

But it was not until they were cycling through the grubby outskirts of Glasgow, past the seemingly endless rows of ugly, identical brick houses enlivened only by an occasional corner pub, that either of them realized how close at hand was their hour of parting, how near to an end their journey together.

And so they were once more in a railway station, this time St Enoch's, enduring the same smoke and grime and eternal railroad noises and rush of people and porters and soldiers with clanking accoutrements, the roll and rumble of baggage trucks and the senseless effeminate shrieking of the eternally hysterical locomotives.

Jerry had bought everything for Patches he could possibly think of – lunch, a bottle of wine and a precious half-bottle of brandy, a box of chocolates, three detective novels, magazines, four packets of Player's cigarettes – and was still prowling around the central bookstall looking for other things to buy her.

Now that the moment was almost at hand, it seemed queer to be saying good-bye to Patches, to be putting her aboard a train that would take her away. But it was not really saying good-bye. She was only going to Kenwoulton, and he would see her again there, at the dances, or in town, perhaps even. . . .

His thoughts stopped there, because he kept seeing the figure of Lester Harrison at the bar of the officers' club and hearing him say: 'Pals while you're together, but when it's finished, that's that. Most of 'em are hundred per cent. No tears, no trouble. Boom, it's over! . . .'

He stole a look at Patches. She was burned brown, and her grey eyes looked light and luminous against the healthy tan of her cheeks. There was a new lustre to the off shade of her hair, now coiled at the back of her neck, hair that he knew was as soft as the finest silk and as fragrant as May flowers. She had changed in the room he had taken at the hotel, and was wearing the same skirt and dark silk blouse in which she had met him. There seemed to be a faraway look in her eyes, but for once her soft, restless, mobile mouth was expressionless. He could not tell what she might be thinking.

Now he had found her a place in a first-class carriage, and he was standing on the platform, looking up at her as she leaned out of the window, and there were five minutes yet to wait until the train should depart, and they did not know what to say to each other.

Patches fought valiantly and gallantly against the tears that lay so close to the surface and yet that must be suppressed until she was alone, because that was how Jerry had wanted it. She had erected, as barriers against shedding them, the unforgettable memories of the hours of beauty they had passed together, but she knew they could not stand against the longing and the loneliness that would come later.

To help her, she called upon the sense of remembered reality of the gloomy station, the familiar sights and sounds and smells, things she had been used to all her life when she went away on trips.

She looked down at this dark boy with the crumpled cap on the back of his glossy head, and the young blue eyes beneath the heavily marked brows, the cleft chin and the gay, careless mouth – this Jerry, who was a piece of her heart, whose heartbeat she had felt, whose being she had shared, whose body had been there to touch when she stirred and reached out in the night – and told herself that it was just someone she knew, almost a stranger, come down to see her off.

They had kissed good-bye on the platform, but it had not hurt too much then, for it had been but a brushing kiss and a hurried hug in the crowd rushing for places in the carriages.

Jerry smiled up. 'See you when I get back to Kenwoulton. . . .'

Patches said: 'Have a good time, Jerry.'

'You've been wonderful, Patches. . . .'

Closing carriage doors banged down the line. The whistle

shrieked twice. Patches gave Jerry her hand, and they gripped for a moment until the train began to move and parted them.

'Good-bye, Patches. . . .'

'God bless, Jerry. . . .'

Far down the station the engine wheezed and chuffed under its load of cars – 'Hundred per cent – hundred per cent – hundred per cent. . . .' The clacking wheels picked up in acceleration, and said faster and faster 'Boom – it's – over! Boom – it's over! Boom – it's – over!' The train was gone from the platform, and the engine, far out in the yards, wailed its farewell: 'I under-sta-a-a-a-nd. . . .'

Jerry watched until the platform was quite empty and the last car had vanished. He sighed and thought: 'Well, I guess that's that. Gee, she was a swell kid. It'll be funny not to have her around. . . .'

He thought of what Major Harrison had said – 'Hell, you don't want to get involved with them!' – put his cap on the back of his head, and walked the streets moodily back to his hotel, where he found himself hesitating to go up to his room. He could not tell whence the feeling had come, but it was as though he knew suddenly that she would be there waiting for him. He pulled himself together and got into the lift.

It was the same kind of high, dark chamber they had occupied together their first night in Glasgow. He closed the door and switched on the single electric drop-light that hung from the ceiling, and the room was so filled with her presence that he stood for a moment blinking at the emptiness as though there were something wrong.

He saw her first only in odd little things she had left behind: a tiny blue pin set with baby turquoises, a powder box on the edge of the wash-stand, a crumpled empty packet of Player's cigarettes – she preferred them to the American brand he smoked – and an inner sole that had come loose and fallen out of one of her slippers.

She had promised him right from the beginning that she was untidy. Jerry, trained to finicky neatness in the Air Force, had instituted something called 'Policing Quarters,' in which they were supposed to share, but which always ended up with Patches sitting cross-legged on the bed smoking a cigarette and pointing out things he was overlooking – 'Oh, Jerry, there – over in the corner. Why do I like to throw things in corners?' while Jerry picked them up and muttered threats of extraordinary Air Force punishments and gigs.

He went about the room picking things up, as though Patches were indeed sitting on the bed, and when he had them all in a little pile, he stood looking at them with a puzzled frown that they should be there and not Patches. She always had difficulty in closing the pin, and he seemed to hear her muttering: 'Oh, bother!' until he came over and fixed it for her.

And she had her own little way of putting powder on her nose and then holding it up to him for inspection. And he would kiss her on the tip as a signal that it was all right.

The inner sole had long been loose from the slipper and was always coming out and being put back in again, because shoes in England were hard to come by, and they would try to think of stopping to get some glue and paste it. And nightfall would catch them somewhere along the line of their trip with the sole coming loose again, and Patches would groan: 'Oh, dear, we didn't get the glue again! And we were right *in* the shop!'

He took the tiny slip of soft leather in his fingers and held it there for a moment; and then he said her name: 'Patches. . . .'

The sense of missing her, the longing for her presence, overwhelmed him so suddenly that he sat down on the edge of the bed and put his face in his hands and was frightened by the power of the emotion, afraid to look up again at the shattering emptiness of the room because it would verify that Patches was gone.

Physically she was no longer there, but memories of her crowded in upon him – her voice, expressions of her face, the feel of her cheek against his, the odd independence of her little toe, her laugh, the shape of her fingernails, the soft and trusting warmth of her sleeping, and a hundred other things he did not even know he had noted.

He said: 'Oh, Christ, no!' and got up from the bed jerkily and went to the window and looked out upon the traffic in the street below and saw a girl on a bicycle who reminded him of the erect, excited way that Patches rode, her little head and eager eyes turning this way and that so as to be sure to miss nothing.

Hell, it was just that he had got used to her, she was such a sweet little kid! The thing to do was to stop acting like a baby and go downstairs and have a couple of drinks and forget the whole business. If every guy who ever had a little adventure with a girl moped around when it was over until. . . .

His eyes fell on his Valpack, with his name and rank stencilled on the side, and at once he felt the pang of missing the fat little bag that belonged to Patches, and the thought came to him that he wasn't every guy. He was Jerry Wright, and somehow what seemed to go for other men didn't go for him. He wasn't like Major Harrison, or even like Sam Bognano. And then as he sat down again on the bed with a dreadful feeling of being drained and lost and empty, he realized that in many ways he wasn't even Jerry Wright any more. He was a part of someone else who was no longer there, the someone who was called Patches.

And once the thoughts began, and the beginnings of truth

pierced his understanding, there was no stopping them. There could be no forgetting Patches, ever. She was under his skin. She was in his heart, his mind, his soul, and his senses for all time.

He sat staring before him, unseeing but remembering so many of the things that had seemed to be no more than pauses on the way to sensual ecstasy.

And he knew now that each and every one was intimately connected with Patches. The young breasts were the tender, swelling, lovable breasts of Patches, and not the mere stimulating and exciting paps of women. They were so completely and extraordinarily hers in shape and form and proportioned to her body – the velvet skin and softly budded tips, her carriage of them and the tenderness with which she yielded them to him. No one but Patches could have done it so or made him such a sweet and gentle gift.

The small, warm movements of her body approaching the anguish of climax were hers, and the sounds in her throat, the trembling of her soft lips, and the utterly dear fragrance of her hair and skin – these were as much a part of Patches as her voice, her smile, or the wrinkling of her nose when she laughed.

Jerry was thinking now of the emotion that had been growing in him all through the wonderful days and nights with Patches and that he had struggled so to suppress. He recalled moments when she had been in his arms, her body welded to his in mutual passion, when he had been so deeply moved and shaken by the sweetness of her that he had wanted to whisper to her: 'Patches, Patches! I love you, oh, I love you! ...' He had never permitted himself to do so.

He could say it now, as well as feel it throbbing in his heart – now that she was gone and the inescapable meaning of their union became at last clear to him. For they were wedded to each other. A marriage had taken place, in and around and about them; this thing that happened between a man and a woman to unite them and bind them to each other in union permeated them; this was the full fragrance and flower of the love that can be brought into being between a man and a woman.

The tall, drab room became a kind of torture chamber to Jerry, a prison of mirrors where the very walls and ceiling and doors and the drab furniture reflected the truths that were welling up from deep inside him.

You could play at being a man, go through the outward motions of a gay and lighthearted adventure, a careless holiday to be put away as an episode of a war-torn world turned upside down, but what if you found that afterward the presence of the girl had entered into your bloodstream, that the touch of her hand on yours, the texture of her skin, the expression of her eyes, the feel and smell of her hair, the sound of her voice, were as necessary to you as the air you breathed and the food that sustained you?

What could you do, how could you forget, if you knew every bright corner of her dear mind, the little human likes and dislikes, the generosities and tendernesses and capacities for love and sympathy? Patches had kept nothing back in the hours they had played and lived and talked together. She had showed him the gentle, dreamy other world in which she lived, and permitted him to enter in and share it with her. She had concealed neither her weakness nor her strength, and in his mind there was now a memory of her of such simple, human, lovable beauty that he felt as though he could not bear it, and he said aloud what he could no longer deny: 'Patches ... Patches, I love you. . . .'

It was then, with shame flushing his face and an icy feeling at the pit of his stomach, that Jerry saw himself and what he had done; that he had made a bawd of her and sent her away alone without ever revealing what was in his heart for her, without letting her know the things he felt.

He had sent her away, this girl to whom he was wedded, who completed him and filled every corner of his being, with a wave and a handshake and a careless thank you, like a prostitute from whom he bought favours, in fulfilment of a standard of behaviour that was supposed to be grown-up and manly.

He had set the terms baldly and brutally in accordance with how he had been told the game was played, and Patches had met them to the very end. He was remembering her as he had last seen her framed in the window of the railway carriage, so small and game, dry-eyed, her head held high, her hand raised to wave until she was out of sight.

'Most of 'em are hundred per cent. No tears and no trouble. Boom, it's over!'

But what did you do if it wasn't over inside you? If it could never be over, if you knew that as long as you lived and wherever you were, the memory of her and the longing to have her next you would be with you?

Jerry's eyes fell upon his Valpack, as from below, a migrant locomotive emitted its piercing wail, and he knew what he must do, what he was impelled to do for his salvation, if there was to be any future, any life thereafter.

Hurry! Go down to the station. Catch the night train. Squeeze in somewhere. Go back. Hurry home to Kenwoulton to find Patches and take her in his arms, to hold her to him and see her beloved head and eyes again and the little fluttering at the corners of her mouth, to tell her that he loved her, to beg her to forgive him, and plead with her to marry him, never again to leave him.

He leaped up from the bed, and the scramble to pack his

bag gave momentary relief to his nerves and feelings until the dreadful doubt as to what Patches would say and do entered his mind. What if she didn't love him? What if the trip had not meant as much to her as it had to him, if it had been just a gay adventure to her? Surely if she had loved him she would have cried a little at the parting, given some sign. . . .

Doubt and fear made him fumble and redouble his efforts, and he struggled with his alarm, calling up memories of moments together and preparing in his mind what he would say to her when he found her, all the things that had cried to be said before – 'Patches, I love you so much. You must love me. You've got to marry me, Patches, you've got to. There's nothing in the whole world, nobody but. . . .'

Jerry stopped in the middle of his packing, sat down on a chair with his hands clutching his head, and said: 'Oh, Christ! I must be going crazy.' He had thought of Catharine.

He had never quite forgotten her, but she had drifted into the background as the world each had known had receded more and more from Patches and him during the romantic, tender period of their honeymoon.

Catharine was there now. She lived. She existed. He was engaged to her. At that very moment she might be reading and rereading the letter he had written her at the completion of his thirtieth mission two weeks ago. He had hinted that the time was not far off when they would be able to get married.

Catharine . . . Patches . . . love . . . marriage . . . Tell Patches: 'I love you, there's nobody on earth but you,' and hear her say: 'What about the girl you were going to marry at home, Jerry?' He couldn't even speak to Patches, much less go to her. He wasn't free. He was Lieutenant Jerry Wright of Westbury, Long Island, and the U.S. Army Air Forces, an officer and a gentleman, engaged to be married to Miss Catharine Quentin in St

John's Episcopal Church in Westbury ... orange blossoms and floating tulle, Sam Bognano for his best man, bridesmaids in organdie, their parents in the front row, her mother weeping a little, rice at the church door and wedding breakfast at the club. ...

Patches ... Catharine ... Jerry wrestled. Walk up the aisle with Catharine, with Patches in his heart? Go back to Kenwoulton and the airbase, be close to Patches, see her, feel her presence, and never speak? Write and destroy Catharine? Keep his promise and marry Catharine, and never for a moment escape from the memory of and desperate longings for Patches?

There was no answer he could find, no escape, no plan. He left his bag where it was, open in the middle of the room, put on his cap and went downstairs, and, only half seeing, crossed the street to the Grosvenor Saloon Bar opposite the station, where he found a place at the bar and ordered a double brandy.

A big American ATC pilot, who with his back turned had made room, looked around at him, stared and said: 'Well, pluck all my feathers and call me baldy! Jerry Wright, you little bastard, you! What are you doing up here among the haggis and the thistle?'

Jerry put his drink down. It was Eagles Wilson, the Air Transport pilot who had played full back on the Westbury High School team when Jerry was an end. They hugged each other – it had been three years since they had last met, and for a moment, seeing Eagles was like a breath of home to Jerry, and yet in the next instant he felt he hardly knew what to say to him. He tossed off his double brandy, to try to pull himself together, and ordered another, and explained that he was on the tag end of a rest furlough and still had five days to go. He added: 'I was going out to Prestwick to look you up.'

'Well, whaddya know? What a break! I'm just having a

quickie beer before driving out there. I've got a jeep. We're taking off in a couple of hours with a V.I.P., and I mean a *very* important personage. Come on out and meet the gang.'

Quite suddenly Jerry didn't want to go. It was good to see Eagles, but somehow he couldn't face a gang of pilots. He needed to be alone. The pain that was torturing him was very close to the surface.

He ordered another double brandy at ten shillings and drew a look from the barmaid. He said to Eagles: 'Have another.'

The big pilot shook his head and said: 'Not me. I'm driving. Non-stop to New York. A *very* important personage.' Then he added casually: 'Kinda soaking it up, aren't you, kid?'

Jerry didn't reply, but tossed the drink off at a gulp and set the glass down on the bar with a sharp click that made him frown. He tried to signal the barmaid, but she ignored him pointedly and busied herself with trade at the other end of the bar.

Eagles said: 'Come on, kid, let's go. We got a lot to talk about,' and took Jerry by the arm and led him to the jeep parked outside.

They started out of town on the twenty-five mile drive to Prestwick, and Eagles drove silently, threading the jeep through the traffic until they were out in the rolling country. Then he remarked, apropos of nothing: 'Kinda longing for that girl of yours, aren't you, kid?'

Jerry looked up startled. How could Eagles guess what was gnawing ceaselessly at his vitals? Did it show on one's face like that?

Eagles continued: 'I don't blame you. Catharine's one in a million. She's a hundred per cent. I saw her the last time I was home. Damn if she hasn't gotten more beautiful! She's all for you, kid.'

III

Jerry's face twitched, and when he spoke, his voice was hoarse. He said: 'Yeah, Cat's a wonderful girl. . . .'

They drove on a little in silence. Then Eagles asked: 'How'd you like to pay her a little visit?'

Jerry looked up with a trace of irritation and said: 'What the hell are you talking about? I'm due back at Gedsborough on Tuesday.' This was Friday.

Eagles replied loftily, and with a trace of mock dramatics: 'Think nothing of it. Since when has time and space been an obstacle to an intrepid birdman?' He changed his tone of banter and said: 'Look here, kid. There's nothing the matter with you that a look into that girl's eyes won't fix. Here's this V.I.P. job. It's a turn-around. We lay over eight hours in New York and come right back. We'll be back here Sunday. One of our guys will drop you off at Gedsborough on his way to London, and you'll have two days to spare, if that's what you're worrying about.'

Jerry was staring at him. Eagles laughed. 'Scared? Hell! The guys do it all the time. I've got a C-87. It's a sleeper jump.'

Jerry's mind was spinning. Home . . . Catharine . . . a sleeper jump. . . . Even to a Bomber pilot used to tooling his tin goose on a twelve-hundred-mile round trip to drop his eggs, home was a place that was aeons away from Gedsborough Airbase, separated by ocean, time, and distance – and fifty missions.

The hangar buildings and the low, flat concrete plains of the ocean air-lanes terminus at Prestwick began to loom up in the distance. Prestwick! Next stop La Guardia Field! Home lay just beyond those low, curved grey buildings. . . .

Now his mind began to race. He would be able to see Catharine. Talk to her face to face. Go to her and tell her what had happened, make her understand. She must understand if he had a chance to talk to her, to tell her how it was and how he felt about Patches. Those things happened to men. What could not be set down coldly on paper could be spoken face to face. It was the decent way to do it. Catharine would realize and set him free – free to go back to Patches, to storm up the grim alley of Bishop's Lane and push the button under the name, 'Sgt P. Graeme, WAAF', and go in and shout up the stairs: 'Patches ... Patches. I'm back ... I've got to see you. ...'

She wouldn't even know he'd been away, that he'd been to America and back to fetch his freedom and the right to beg her to marry him, to tell her what was in his heart. But she would know what was there when he plucked her off the stairs and held her to him. ...

Eagles said: 'Sold?'

'You're sure ... we'd get back on Sunday? ...'

Eagles snorted: 'Huh! Or else! I've told you it's a *very important* personage. ...'

He might be back in Kenwoulton by Sunday night saying to Patches: 'I'm free. I'm not engaged, Patches. There's nobody. but you. ...' It was fate that he had run into Eagles that way, fate that Eagles was flying a round trip, fate that meant him to have his chance to speak to Catharine. ...

They were at the entrance to Prestwick and showing their A G O cards to the M.Ps.

Eagles said: 'That's all, brother. I can see it on your face. It's what the doctor ordered. Now look, stick around close to me and just don't talk to anyone and you won't have to tell any lies. Go aboard when I do. It's my ship, and nobody will ask any questions. I'll let you have one more schnapps before we go if you think you need it.'

'To hell with it!' said Jerry, 'I don't. Eagles, you're the tops! ...'

Jerry sat up in the nose of the C-87 with Eagles as, with the four motors drumming, the concrete floor of Prestwick slipped away beneath them and the blue waters of the Firth of Clyde appeared below, with the Isle of Arran a green patch to the north.

Ireland passed beneath them and was gone. They climbed into the high clouds, and soon, through the rifts, there was nothing but the sea below. Eagles set the automatic pilot and checked with his engineer. He said to Jerry: 'Take a snooze, sonny. I'll wake you when we pass the Statue of Liberty. . . .'

'Sleep!' said Jerry. 'My God, are you crazy? . . .'

He wondered what his mother and father would say. . . .

2

THE big ship came in from the sea and lazed down Long Island, and the familiar panorama spread beneath Jerry's eyes – Jericho Turnpike, farmlands that were cut and fenced like the chequerboard fields of England, Mitchell and Roosevelt with the landmark of the big gas tank, then the curve of Flushing Bay and the grey asphalt surface and gleaming buildings of La Guardia Airport.

The engines, throttled down, were whistling, sighing, and popping as they circled for a landing. What lay below was so well known, so much a part of him, and yet Jerry was not stirred. He was standing up in the pilot's compartment of the ship, his eyes picking up the flat, concrete administration building, judging the distance with Eagles, bringing the ship in with him in his mind – another airport, another landing. . . .

Markers, trucks, men digging at the side of the runway flashed by. The wheels touched; the ship settled and rolled. The engines picked up, and they taxied to the main building, where a car with motor-cycle escort awaited the Very Important Personage, who left the plane and entered his conveyance hugging a brief-case to him.

Eagles looked at his watch. It was four o'clock in the afternoon. He said: 'On the nose! You can get a cab right outside in a few minutes. Need any money? Here, better take twenty until you get home. They don't understand about pounds over here yet. Be back here at two in the morning. I'll meet you at the information centre. Then you can stick around with me until we go aboard. Okay, kid, good luck! And give her a big kiss for old Eagles. . . .'

Jerry drifted into the rotunda of the main passenger hall. He walked as if in a dream, past the news-stands, where well-remembered New York newspapers flashed the big headlines of the war; people, his kind of people, sat, or sauntered, or rushed behind porters carrying their bags. Over the loud-speaker system a woman's voice announced: 'American Airlines, the Southwesterner, for Washington, Nashville, and Dallas, Texas, now loading at gate three.'

Only yesterday he had heard the same kind of voice, but speaking in a cool, clipped British accent, announcing: 'London Express, for Carlisle, Manchester, Stoke, Birmingham, Northampton, and London, now ready at platform one.' That was the train on which Patches had gone back.

He passed a row of telephone booths and hesitated. Should he call up home and tell them he was coming? He felt no urge to do so, no sensation of being within a telephone call of his mother and father and Catharine. A five-cent piece, a number spoken into the mouth-piece would have verified it. But he could not bring himself to cross the threshold. It was almost as if by doing so he would have destroyed the spell.

Jerry went out to the entrance through a door marked 'TAXIS'. A Yellow, with a long hood, looking enormous and ornate with dilapidated gimcrackery, lamps, and ornaments, pulled up to him from the head of the line. Like the newspapers and the people and the talk he was hearing, it was familiar and a part of him. And yet he could not quite penetrate the still dreamlike quality of his being there. The cab made him think of a circus wagon he had once seen in Westbury as a child.

He got in and gave the address, 12 Severn Avenue, Westlake

Park. The driver looked around. 'Cost ya a fin, bud. I gotta come back empty.'

'That's okay.'

The driver set the cab in motion and headed for the parkway that would take them out on the island. When they were rolling, he half turned his head and asked: 'Well, how's things over there?'

Jerry said: 'Over where?' and meant it. His body had been transported to America, but his mind had not yet made the transition. He had been thinking of Gedsborough Airbase, Sam Bognano, his ship, and the crew.

The driver said: 'On the other side. Ain't you just back from there? I see by them ribbons you got on. . . . I got a kid in the Pacific. How's it – pretty tough?'

Jerry replied: 'It gets a little rugged sometimes.' He looked at the photograph and name of the driver on the identification placard inside the cab. It was Edgerton Bibber, Long Island City. The last time he had been in a cab had been a fortnight ago in London with Sam Bognano, his pilot. They had gone to a night club in one of the tiny-bonneted, high-fashioned London taxis, driven by a cockney who had a son with the Eighth Army in Italy. There had been a V alert on at the time, but the cabby paid it no mind and told them about driving all through the blitz of '40.

The driver of the Yellow remarked: 'I guess you fellers get a bellyful. . . .'

Jerry did not reply. His mind was impaled upon something he could not catch. Then it came – the name of the driver. Patches would have loved it, and would have started to make a song about it. They had collected odd names seen on shop fronts and hotel registers all through their trip together. There was one in particular he remembered they had come upon at

117

Stronachlachar, a gentleman by the name of Peabody Twitillie, and they had cycled to its refrain for hours.

Jerry started a couplet – 'Oh, Edgerton Bibber, he was a . . .' But it wouldn't come. It wasn't any good without Patches. Nothing was any good without Patches. That's why he was bowling along Grand Central Parkway in a taxi-cab to go and talk to Catharine and get straightened out.

He had to get a grip on himself, to put his hand down and feel the leather of the seat and look up again at the name placard of the driver and beyond to the familiar traffic of the parkway. Home and Catharine were beyond, and Patches had only just pulled out of St Enoch's Station, wearing that silly little hat with the blue cornflowers on it, and holding up her hand to him, framed in the window of the railway carriage until she was out of sight.

In Jerry's mind the coughing of the taxi motor turned into the chuff-chuff-chuff of the long, packed train as it snaked its way out of the station in Glasgow; he no longer saw the parkscape of Long Island, but only the grey canopy of the terminus and the gap left by the departed train. 'Chuff-chuff-chuff,' and then the mournful shriek of those damned English locomotive whistles. He'd never get the sound out of his ears.

Patches ought to be in Kenwoulton by now, back to the dismal, lightless brick house in Bishop's Lane, with the chimney pots like rabbit's ears – back to the war, back where she started from with her fat little bag and her wistful, shadowy smile. It was there at the foot of the stairs that she had looked at his watch and timed the beginning of their adventure together. He wondered whether she would glance at the time again and note when it was ended. . . . The cab reached the end of the parkway and swung off. Only a few more miles. Oh, God, he was in a mess! . . .

When they approached Westbury on the Jericho Turnpike, Jerry said to the driver: 'Never mind taking me to that address. Drop me on the edge of town somewhere. I'll tell you when. . . .'

'Whatever you say, bud. Guess you don't want to walk in on 'em too sudden, eh?'

Jerry let it go at that. Actually now that he was nearing Westbury and passing over roads every inch of which he had traversed in his jalopy when he was a kid, he wanted more time to think, to get acclimatized to being back, to rid himself of the dream fabric that seemed to enfold him like a mantle. He had the queer feeling that if he came banging up the house in a cab, slamming the door, he would wake everyone. He wished now that he had telephoned. Sometime the queer illusion must break, sometime he must find himself at home. . . .

Half-way through Westbury he tapped on the window. 'This will do right here.' He got out and dismissed the cab at the corner of Main and Chestnut opposite the high school.

The street was filled with Saturday-afternoon shopping traffic. Through the store window he could see Joe the shine man giving the final gloss to a patron's shoes with the characteristic flamboyant flip of his polishing rag. Next door was Malloy's, the candy store where he and Catharine would stop for some ice cream after the movies. Down the street the Bijou Theatre marquee advertised a picture he had seen six months ago at Gedsborough Airbase. Templeton's market, where his mother used to send him on his bicycle to pick up something the delivery boy had forgotten, was jammed with people picking over the vegetables and fruits. He recognized Herbert the fat groceryman tearing off the greens from bunches of carrots.

Under the noise of motor traffic and the squawks of a swing band from Milt's radio shop, he could hear the thudding of ball against racket gut from the tennis courts at the side of the high school. Looking up at the high school, he could see the windows of the chem. lab. were open and figures moving about or bending over, kids working overtime on a problem late Saturday afternoon. . . . The showcase of Pappos the florist was full of blue hydrangea plants, and Jerry remembered that his mother liked them. The air smelled of expensive cars and caramel popcorn from Malloy's and gasoline and summer sun on pavements, and still he was not at home. . . .

His mind was turning back to Kenwoulton with a queer kind of yearning for the ugly red-brick buildings with their bomb gaps, odour of bitter beer when you passed a pub, the persistent peat-smoke smell that hung in the air, the drab queues waiting at the bus signs, the tobacco shops with their green- and red-coloured packets of cigarettes and tins of tobacco, old newsmen hawking the London papers, apple-cheeked slatterns gossiping in front of the butcher shops or standing in line at the fishmongers', startling and yet amusing his ears with the off-key music of their Midlands burr.

It wasn't that he liked Kenwoulton, or even England. He had felt exiled there like the rest of the kids, and thought only of home, talked of it, longed for it, counted each mission, each day that brought him nearer to it. It was more that his mind, confused and harried by the events of the past forty-eight hours, was searching for surroundings where he would not feel a stranger, where he could feel comfortable. He had never so much as consciously looked at Kenwoulton when he had been in that dismal, ugly Midlands manufacturing town, but now his memory of it was suddenly sharp and filled with warmth. And it was the place where Patches would be. . . .

Jerry saw no one he knew; no one appeared to recognize him. There was no one who expected to see him standing there. He was just a young Air Force officer, another soldier of many who were a part of the afternoon traffic, but it gave Jerry the strangest feeling that he was invisible, that he did not exist as a corporeal body, that physically he was not really there at all.

He turned slowly and walked up the street towards the road that would lead him the half-mile to Severn Avenue and home. A block away he saw the familiar porticoed front of the public library and the building of St John's Episcopal Church next to it. A girl came out of the library with some books under her arm, and something about her swinging walk and slender figure made him stop and stare.

He was saying to himself: 'It's Catharine,' as though this were part of the dream too and he was identifying someone. Even this queer inability to move was dreamlike, a remembered fantasy out of the night when the body became suddenly heavy and leaden and refused to obey the dictates of the mind. Catharine – within his sight, within his reach. With a curious pang he saw her sunny smile flash as she recognized an acquaintance on the way to her car at the kerb and paused a moment to talk.

Jerry moved slightly, half into the doorway of the stationery shop, and was startled to find that his limbs still retained the power of locomotion. Then why was he not running forward down the street to Catharine? A crying of her name, a shout of greeting, a wave of his arm, and she would look up and see him coming towards her. Old habits, old memories, days and nights of longing to see her, of thinking about her, were strongly impelling him, and yet he remained where he was.

Then through the confusion and turmoil in his mind a stronger power penetrated the chaos within him like a sombre undertone – the remembrance of the reason for his presence there, the purpose of his mission – and he felt suddenly like a traitor. He thought at once of Patches, and she came so alive in his mind that for a moment he felt like a traitor to both.

Time seemed to hang suspended while he waited, and he had the feeling that at any instant Catharine would feel his presence, would look up and come to him. But she did not. She chatted for a moment and then moved on to her car, her books under her arm. For her, Jerry was three thousand miles away, no closer than his latest letter, which she carried in her handbag. Even had she glanced down the block in his direction, she might not have recognized him shielded in the doorway, because in her thoughts he was so firmly placed in England.

Still motionless, Jerry watched her climb into her roadster and drive away towards home, her hair blowing out behind her, and his thoughts went back to the daydreams he used to have during the long, dreary hours on their way to and from missions when there was no enemy attack and he would soothe his nerves and pass the time with fantasies of how it would be to come back to Catharine again, what their meeting would be like, and where, and how.

In his mind he had gone over them all, placing it in New York, perhaps at the airport, or at the little railway station of Westbury, or even at the door of her home, beneath the tall elms and the lilac bushes, and his yearnings would always culminate in the moment when she would run into his outstretched arms and he would feel her hair against his cheek, and the tender touch of her mouth, confirming for all time the promise they had made to each other before he left.

And as he stood there he realized that the moment had come and gone, and that he was no longer the same Jerry Wright who had left Westbury two years ago with his new wings on his breast and Catharine in his heart, and never would be again. And he had a sudden longing for his home, his father and mother, his room and his things. He left the doorway and began to walk rapidly.

He took a back way to Severn Avenue so as to avoid the necessity of passing Catharine's house across the street from his. Coming around from behind, he walked the short gravel driveway, and, standing inside the white-columned Georgian portico, he pressed the button of the bell.

Deep inside the house he heard the well-remembered sound of the vibration and a sharp bark, and for the first time he had the feeling that the dream shroud was breaking up, that he was indeed a living person.

The touch of his finger upon the bell, the sounds, the entrance with the polished brass letter box, the nick in the woodwork he had made with his hockey stick when he had slipped there one winter's day, the familiar feel of the worn, thick mat beneath his feet – seemed to bring him back and give promise of the dear objects that lay just behind those walls. . . .

Reston the butler opened the door, stared, and fell out of all calm and order. His eyes started, his stout face flushed red as he cried:

'*Mister* Jerry! Bless me!'

There was a wild scrabbling of toenails on polished hardwood floor, and Skipper, Jerry's golden cocker, precipitated himself upon him and into his arms, yelping and screaming, licking his face hysterically. A door opened above and a woman's voice called: 'Reston! What is it? Is there something the matter?'

Jerry went to the foot of the stairs and called up: 'Mother . . .'

'Jerry! Jerry! Oh no, I can't believe it! Harman, do you hear! It's Jerry. Jerry's back. . . .'

Helen Wright came running down the stairs, and Jerry took her in his arms and hugged her and let her cry and kiss him. His father came down, wiping shaving-soap from his face, shouting: 'Jerry! Why didn't you let us know? By God, let's look at you, son!'

He was home now. It was what he had thought it would be like seeing his father and mother – their excitement, surprise, and joy, Reston's pop eyes, and the hysterical Skipper. He grinned at them. 'I just landed forty-five minutes ago, and thought I'd come right out. Gee, Mother, you look great! Dad, you're a sight for sore eyes, even with only half your whiskers off.'

Helen Wright was saying over and over: 'Jerry, Jerry, darling! ... I just cannot believe it.' She was a small, nervous, somewhat breathless woman, with a still handsome face and figure, expressive eyes, and a way of making herself the centre of things. For all that hers had been a perfect marriage, blessed with an adoring and indulging husband and a fine son, she was always girding herself for the effort of coming to grips with little things.

Her husband was feasting his eyes on Jerry's ribbons, his features flushed with excitement and pride. He was an older and more firmly settled edition of Jerry, with the same dark, glossy hair and blue eyes, and the pink-and-white complexion of a man for whom everything had gone right. His figure in his silk dressing-gown was heavier but as trim and well-muscled as Jerry's. There was no doubt that they were father and son, though they might have been taken for brothers.

He said: 'By God, son, D.F.C., Air Medal, Silver Star, you've got 'em all, and thank goodness, no Purple Heart! ...'

Helen stood off to contemplate him better. 'Jerry, you're taller – and better-looking. Is it really true you're here? I simply cannot wait to hear about you. We had a letter from you only yesterday. And look at Skipper, he's turning himself inside out. ...'

They went into the library, where Jerry smelled the old familiar scent of leather and books and said: 'Oh gee, it's good to be home!'

His father said: 'You'll find everything in your room exactly as you left it. Son, I'm so pleased and excited at having you back I don't know where to begin, and I guess Mother feels the same way. Let's get our breath and hear all about it. . . .'

'Tell us everything, Jerry, how long you . . .' Helen Wright paused in the middle of the sentence and then exclaimed: 'Catharine! Jerry, does Catharine know you're home? Of course not, if you came right here. Don't you want to call her right away? I'm sure she's at home. . . .'

Jerry looked at his mother. In the pleasure of being there, the genuine joy he felt at seeing his parents, he momentarily had forgotten everything else. Now he thought: 'Oh, Lord . . . it's got to come! . . .'

Helen was making plans, sharing in the romance of the moment when Jerry and Catharine would be together again. She said: 'Of course you'll want to go over there first. Oh, Jerry, you ought to prepare her – it's only fair. Let me call Millicent and just hint. . . .' In her excitement she had moved half-way to the telephone when Jerry said: 'Mother – don't . . . please . . . I mean . . .'

His father said: 'Jerry probably has his mind made up just how he's going to spring it on Cat, Mother. . . . It's just that we're so damned excited at your walking in this way, son. . . .'

Jerry faced them both, and his tone was serious and troubled. He said: 'Look, I guess you'll think I'm pretty screwy for doing it, but I'm not really back at all. I'm flying out again at two o'clock tomorrow morning. I was on leave in Scotland and ran into a guy – remember Eagles Wilson? He was flying a V.I.P. on a seventy-two-hour turn-around. I went along for the ride.'

Harman Wright threw back his head and laughed lustily. 'By God, what a war! A.W.O.L., eh?'

'Well, not exactly, except I'm not supposed to be in this country. My leave isn't up until Wednesday. I'll be back in Scotland Sunday night.'

Helen slumped into a chair and said: 'Oh dear, I'm sure I just can't bear any more. Jerry, you'll be the death of us.' She stiffened suddenly. 'But, Jerry, that's all the more reason for your seeing Catharine at once. She'll be so happy – and so disappointed. Oh, I want to be with you every minute you're here, but we can understand, can't we, Harman?'

Harman Wright was looking at his son, looking beyond the clean young figure to the shadows on his face and the eyes that did not seem either young or happy. He said, tentatively: 'Why, sure, Jerry. You run along over if you want to. Maybe you can bring Cat back for dinner. . . .'

Jerry was standing in the centre of the room thinking: 'Oh Lord! . . . How am I going to tell them?' Aloud he said: 'I'll go over later, after a while, but I wanted to have a chance to talk to you first. It's on account of Catharine I came home. . . .'

'Jerry!' The note of alarm in his mother's voice filled him with foreboding. 'Is there anything wrong between you and Catharine?'

The emphasis his mother placed upon the question made it pregnant with apprehension of disaster, as though the turning of the wheels of the world depended upon things being right between Catharine and himself, and Jerry for the first time began to have an inkling of the enormity of the trouble he was in and its possible effect upon others. He suddenly felt a thousand years old and a thousand years tired, and his heart swelled with gratefulness when his father said quietly: 'I think a drink might be in order, son. You've had one hell of a long trip!'

He went to the side table, where whisky and soda stood, and poured out a double for his son, noting the gratitude in his eyes and how the boy's hand shook when he took it.

Jerry sat across a chair and leaned forward on the backrest, as he always had, trying to think what to say. His father suggested quietly: 'Tell us about it if you feel like it, Jerry. . . .'

It was his mother who was worrying Jerry, the fidgeting of her fingers and the frightened look on her face. He said: 'There isn't anything wrong. . . . I mean I haven't seen her yet to talk to her. It's . . . well, I met a girl over in England, and . . .'

'Oh, Jerry, no!'

Helen Wright had spoken the words as though it were the end of the world, and for a moment it made Jerry angry. The hurt, shocked look on her face, the expression of her voice, her emphasis of the words, made him feel the way he had when he was a small boy confessing to something. But his anger faded when he realized that she was deeply distressed.

Harman Wright said nothing, but nursed his drink and studied his son.

A new alarm seized Helen and she cried: 'Jerry, you aren't . . . you haven't . . . ?'

'Married her? No. But I want to. That's why I had to come home and talk to Catharine.'

'Jerry! . . . It isn't true. I can't believe it. You couldn't . . .' There was a hint of hysteria in her voice that frightened Jerry. His father caught it too and asked quietly: 'Who is she, Jerry?'

Who was Patches? What was she, a being, one of the countless millions who occupied a tiny pinpoint of earth somewhere, to be identified with a name and colouring and

127

ancestry, a catalogue of features, a place in society? Or was she the beating of his heart, his hunger and his thirst, his hope on earth?

Ever since they had parted and he knew what she meant to him, he had been groping in his mind for words to express the music of Patches that permeated him, to find release for the things that had come alive within him. And now that his father had asked: 'Who is she?' he could only reply: 'Her name is Patch ... Patrice Graeme. She's in the RAF. She's a radar expert.' Then he added: 'I'm in love with her.'

His mother drew in a deep breath. 'Jerry! How can you say such a thing? It can't be anything but an infatuation. ...'

Jerry winced. He hated the word. He always had ever since he first had heard it. He hated it all the more now because his mother had brought it up in connexion with Patches. It was a word that somehow cheapened things and made him feel less like a man.

His father flicked his cigarette stub into the fireplace with concise accuracy, and said, surprisingly: 'Jerry isn't a child any more, Helen,' and drew a look of gratitude from his son. 'Go on, Jerry. ...'

Jerry said: 'That's all, sir. I didn't want to write. When I met Eagles and had a chance to come home and see you all and try to get straightened out, I took it.'

The disappointment, frustration, and helpless anger that were mounting in Helen Wright were more the result of her perpetual defences reared against any possible threat to the security she had built, and the suddenness with which the crisis had been presented, than due to any lack of sympathy or love for Jerry.

He was still a child to her. She had only the most meagre conception of the war, of the part men were called upon to play, of the kind of life he had been living, or of what he had been called upon to face. The war had taken Jerry from their home. She had not realized how quickly she had substituted Catharine. Beyond the minor annoyances of rationing and the whole-hearted performance of patriotic duties, the holocaust had simply not managed to penetrate her home.

But she loved Catharine Quentin genuinely, and the forthcoming marriage of her son and the daughter of her dearest and oldest friend had been even closer to her heart than she might have realized. And as a woman, she foresaw at once and could even pre-experience vicariously something of the dreadful shock and pain that was to be brought to someone who was young, innocent, loving, and loyal, and who in the years that Jerry had been away had become very much a part of her own life.

She said in a voice that was beginning to shake: 'Jerry, do you realize what this will do to Catharine? I won't even speak of how your father and I will feel....'

Harman Wright said: 'Helen, don't you think –'

'Wait, Harman! That girl loves you, Jerry. To her, the sun rises and sets in you. She is prepared to devote her life to you. Catharine has already become our daughter. Is that nothing to you, because of some strange girl who ...'

Some strange girl! ... The words echoed in his ears. In the night he had held her to his heart. Some strange girl! ... Patches, who had read his soul the time the flyer's horrors had come upon him, and who, without hint or word from him had unerringly divined his need and, like a soldier and dear comrade, had reached across the gulf to help him.... All the books and people and causes, the colours and shapes of earth, the fragrances of living, all the great, and also all the little, things she loved, he knew and loved too. They had laughed and played and made nonsense rhymes together, and had lain awake at night side by side and talked of life and death and where God was to be found in beauty. . . .

'Oh, Jerry, I can't bear to think of it. Tell me it isn't true,' said Helen Wright, and suddenly put her face into her hands and began to sob hysterically.

Jerry got up. He loved his mother. He wanted to go to her, but did not know how. Harman Wright signalled to Jerry and said: 'Maybe you want to wash up a little, son. Afterwards we might have a talk together.'

After Jerry had gone out, Harman Wright went over to his wife and put his hand on her shoulder with considerable tenderness. He said: 'Pull yourself together, Helen. Nothing really final has happened. I understand how you feel.'

She grew quieter under his touch and cried: 'Harman, it's too dreadful! We can't let him. He doesn't realize. He's too young to know his own mind. He's just a child. You know he's loved Catharine all his life. . . .'

Harman Wright was genuinely upset by his wife's distress. His family was more to him than merely a habit. He loved them greatly and wished them above all to be happy. To make them so, he provided all that was physically in his power of luxury and good living, and to this added the formula by which he had lived so long – the best of all possible worlds, in which good triumphed and the wicked were punished – when they were caught at it.

His was a stratum of society that at least liked to live like gentlemen. His way of life was impregnable to change, disaster, or disintegration. He believed in it, in its mission and its tutelary gods – money, business, advertising, and position – all minor but not insignificant deities, assistants and acolytes to the main god, who was a dignified Episcopalian. He believed in it wholly, since it had been very good to him, and associated only with those who believed likewise.

Nevertheless, he had been a captain of artillery in France in 1917–18, and had his memories.

He said: 'The boy's been to war, Helen. A lot of things can happen. Let me handle him. Go and lie down until dinner and don't worry. You'll make yourself ill. I'll have a talk with him. Jerry's O.K. He'll do what's right in the end.'

Jerry looked up as his father came into the library, his shaving completed, and dressed. He wanted and needed to talk to him, for he respected and trusted him. He asked: 'How's Mother?'

Harman Wright replied: 'She's lying down. She doesn't want any dinner. I'm afraid she's pretty unhappy over this, Jerry.'

'I'm sorry, Dad. . . . I wanted to have a chance to talk to you alone first before I said anything, but it . . . sort of all came out.'

Harman went to the side table and made two highballs. 'Women always have to be eased up to a new idea gradually,' he said. 'Cigar?'

Jerry again felt warmed towards his father for the simple and genuine way he created the atmosphere that his son was a boy no longer, his tacit acknowledgement that the things that had happened to him since he had been away had changed their relationship. He felt strongly that his father was a good man.

They lit their cigars and puffed on them for a moment. Then Harman asked: 'When did you say you were going back?'

'I'm due at the airport at two in the morning. I'd better leave here a little before one to be on the safe side. . . .'

'Hmmmm! You're going to have to work fast, son. Do you want to tell me more about it?'

It was still difficult to tell about Patches and himself and how he felt. Jerry could be more articulate with his father, but there were many omissions, things he could not say, things of which he was regretful; others he instinctively felt might be disloyalties to Patches or intrusions upon her privacy.

Words and emotions that came to him to express his love for Patches sounded silly and strained, and he discarded them as quickly as they rose up in his mind. His father was listening quietly, smoking without comment, while Jerry talked, and his very silence placed an added burden upon the telling. He heard himself saying: 'I met her a couple of months ago . . .' and his own mind made the comparison. 'You met her a couple of months ago. And you've known and loved Catharine for as long as you can remember. . . .'

Here, in his own home, in the familiar surroundings of his father's study, he seemed for the first time removed from the immediacy of the things that had been happening to him. But he was still filled with echoes of the days spent with Patches, pictures of her that drifted across his mind, longings, little visions of scenes and moments, and, above all, the ache in his heart, but they had to be reduced to words and the sound of his own voice and the dreadful inadequacy of speech to convey emotion.

He heard himself saying: 'We went off for a holiday together for ten days, up in Scotland. After she went away I realized what had happened, that I was in love with her. I guess I can't help it, Dad. I'll always be in love with her. . . .'

Harman Wright poured out another drink. He had been listening with his mind as well as with his ears, and he thought that he had a clue. He came directly to the point.

'Do you mind if I ask you something, Jerry?'

'Go ahead, Dad.'

'Do you want to marry her because you think you ought to, on account of going away with her?'

'Oh, my God, Dad, no! ...' The thought had never entered Jerry's mind, but it was startling to hear his father say it, and for the moment it seemed to open a kind of gulf between them, as though he had heard a voice out of another generation, an older man trying to warn a boy not to be foolish and do something quixotic for which he would later be sorry. He thought suddenly how curious that there should be no compulsion upon him to marry Patches because of what had been between them, and so much compulsion in his conscience to marry Catharine, who for all was yet a stranger to him. He said: 'I don't even know if she'll marry me, but I've got to ask her, to make her understand. ... How can I tell her if I'm still engaged? I can't make my run until I'm free. Haven't I done enough to her already? ...'

Harman said quietly: 'I was only asking, son. I just wanted to be sure your thinking was clear. It's your own life, and you are going to have to make your own decisions. ...'

He paused, and in the pause Jerry seemed to feel that the momentary gulf was closing once more. He was too deeply concerned with his problems to realize that he was under attack by a man who was divided between love for his son and love for his wife and family and a way of living, that he was in a fight. ...

His father continued, dragging at his cigar between sentences: 'As long as you realize whatever decisions you make will affect not only yourself. ...'

'Gee, Dad, I know. ...'

'They will affect your mother – very deeply, and Catharine and her family. It may change the whole course of that girl's life and do her irreparable damage. They will also affect Patches. From what you say, she would surely make you a good wife, but she'll be a stranger in a strange land. What's the use of kidding ourselves, Jerry? You know that whoever she is, we'll make your wife welcome as our daughter, but it won't ever be the same, will it? Can it? Your mother will get over the shock eventually, but she's only human after all, and her life has been pretty much wrapped up in you two kids.'

Jerry didn't reply. He was feeling cornered, but he did not attribute it so much to what his father was saying, because they were merely echoes of his own thoughts and struggles. He had never really brought them to the surface, but they had been there. He hadn't looked very far beyond his love for Patches and his desperate need of her, because he hadn't wanted to do so. The song of their being together was still too loud in his heart for him to hear the discords.

But he heard them plainly enough now, because his father was speaking, not with emotion, but reasonably. And yet he had also said: 'It's your own life. . . .'

It was not pity for himself he was experiencing, but a kind of despairing rebellion against the forces that had been set in motion against him, forces for which he himself had been partly responsible, and others that had inexorably swept him out of his youth, his life, his home, and his future.

He thought of a phrase spoken by Major Harrison at the bar of the officers' club at Gedsborough Airbase in what now seemed like the long ago – 'Hell, the whole world's upside down, isn't it?' Jerry hadn't asked to be turned upside down, to be spilled out upon a foreign shore, to fly through the icy stratosphere to drop death and destruction on to the earth below. What could a guy do if he was left suspended head down amidst people who still walked right side up?

Patches was not a dream. She had happened to him. Henceforth, though they should never see each other again, his life would never be complete without her, he would never be at peace, never again be himself.

Harman Wright interrupted his thoughts: 'Jerry. . . .'

'Yes, Dad. . . .'

'Do you mind if I tell you a little story? It's about the last war, when I was in France. . . .'

Jerry looked up, wondering what was coming.

Harman Wright looked about him with a half-humorous air, eyeing the closed door to the study before speaking, and even dropping his voice slightly. 'God forbid that your mother ever should hear of this! It was in Paris after the armistice. I was engaged to your mother at the time, though of course she was back in St Louis. . . .'

Jerry listened with the sudden, queer consciousness that he was feeling embarrassed. His father continued: 'There was a little French girl. Her name was Adrienne. She was pretty as a picture. You know those French girls. I met her in a restaurant on the Bois de Boulogne, and we sort of took to one another. She was really beautiful. I guess you might say she was a stunner.

'Well, to make a long story short, we went away together. We went down to a place called Mentone on the Riviera, and stayed there a week, holed up in a hotel. It was really a wonderful experience for a kid like me who'd never been around much. Did you say something?'

Jerry shook his head. His mind was playing him a curious trick and making him see a picture of the hotel, his father in his World War I uniform, and Adrienne, who looked like the girl on a postcard one of the fellows had brought back with him from France. He realized that he was feeling a little sick at the pit of his stomach. . . .

His father continued: 'I was pretty stuck on Adrienne, in fact I guess I was in love with her. We even talked about getting married. When I left for the States I half promised to come back for her, and I guess I meant it at the time.'

Harman shook the ashes from the stub of his cigar and leaned forward a little in his chair. 'Well, Jerry, here we all are. I've never regretted it – never for a moment. I did a lot of thinking after I came home and saw your mother again. That little French girl wasn't easy to forget. She had a lot of ways about her. I married your mother and settled down. I wouldn't have had it any other way!'

Reston knocked on the door and said: 'Dinner is served, sir. And ah, Mrs Wright said she was not feeling well enough to come down. . . .'

Jerry did not feel like eating either. He wished he could find a hole and crawl away into it. Harman said: 'Very well, Reston, we will be there in just a moment,' and when the butler had closed the door, he concluded: 'I've loved your mother dearly, and I always will. We've had a wonderful life together, and I wouldn't exchange it for any other. We belong together. This is our kind of world, and we understand one another, and our ways and the things we have in common mean a great deal to us. That's all, Jerry. . . .'

They went down and ate dinner by candlelight in the walnut-panelled dining-room, and it was the way it had always been – the creamy linen, the soft sheen of old silver, the gloss of the old wood reflecting the tapers, the sigh of the swinging door, and the quiet footfalls of Reston.

Jerry toyed with his food and tried to answer politely his father's inquiries about the war, the life he led, his missions, his decorations, his ship, and his crew. At any other time he would have spilled over, for part of his long-cherished home-coming dream was the telling of tales and the bragging about his gang and his airplane. But he was deeply hurt and bitterly

136

disillusioned with his father because of what he had told him, the story of the little French girl.

He had trusted his father, had exposed his innermost feelings to him because he had believed somehow that the older man had understood him and what he felt about Patches. And all that had happened was that his father had managed to dirty it up. To confide in him an escapade of his own youth that was supposed to parallel what had happened between Patches and himself. A pick-up in a restaurant and a week in a hotel. 'In Paris after the armistice. . . . You know those French girls. . . .' My God, it was like one of those stories you heard in a smoking-car, or when the gang was gathering around after a mission was scrubbed or after chow and cutting loose on Topic A!

He felt more lonely now and cut off than he ever had before, and the ashes of disappointment in his father were bitter in his mouth. He knew now that he could never make him understand that Patches was more than a girl he had grown to love; she was a brother in arms who wore the uniform of her country and had buried her dead, and that too made all the difference in the world. She belonged; she was as much a fighter, valiant and unconquerable, as any of them.

He had heard of the gulf between those at home and the men who had been overseas and in combat. Now he was facing his father and realized that not even the generation who had fought the last war knew about this one, what it was like and what it did to people, how you got to feel when you lived in a country that had been fighting with its back to the wall for four years, where streets and homes were in the front lines and never a day went by but somebody died from bombs, or shells, or fire, or bullets from the air.

Maybe they were English and had queer ways that weren't like your ways, but they were soldiers, every one of them; they wouldn't quit; they had guts, and you loved them like brothers and sisters.

'You know those French girls. . . . I guess you might say she was a stunner. . . . It was really a wonderful experience for a kid like me who'd never been around much. . . .' His father's words still echoed. And brave, tender, gallant Patches, with her soft smile and warm understanding. . . . What was the use of talking? . . .

The two men had been sitting over their coffee, cigars, and brandy. Jerry looked at his watch. It was eight o'clock. Harman noticed Jerry's gesture and said: 'Well, son, have you decided what you want to do?'

Jerry said: 'I'd better call Catharine before I go over there. It's going to be tough. . . .'

He got up heavily for one so young and moved slowly towards the telephone extension beneath the sideboard. It was the way you felt when you had a rotten mission ahead of you, where the whole atmosphere of the briefing had been heavy with coming disaster and loss, where you shut off your mind from all thinking and worked with your muscles, moving your arms and legs and hands forward into whatever was to come, to get it over with.

Harman Wright felt a pang of pity for his son because he knew he was suffering. Jerry was young and game, and a fighter for what he wanted. His father seemed to recognize the kind of people they were in Jerry's slow, inexorable movement forward into something he must have dreaded with all his soul. The boy was honest. He didn't ask for pity, and he didn't shirk. But Harman had not yet given up the fight. He believed more than ever that he was right and Jerry was wrong.

He asked quietly, without moving: 'What are you going to tell Catharine when you see her?'

Jerry turned and looked up at him heavily. He replied: 'About what happened – I've got to ... about Patches and me....'

'Are you going to tell her that you lived together....'

Jerry suddenly cried: 'Oh, Christ, Dad, stop hitting below the belt!' Then he said: 'I'm sorry. I guess not. One doesn't speak about such things. I've got to ask her to let me out. I thought if I told her what Patches means to ...'

He stopped suddenly, because his mind, grown vivid under the impact of the things that had been happening to him, leaped ahead as it were to show him to himself sitting in the chintz-decorated sun-porch off the living-room of the Quentin house with Catharine at his side.

And he saw her there as he had last remembered her – so healthily beautiful, loving, young, vigorous, clear-eyed, innocent, sexless, and inexperienced as ... as he had once been and now was no longer. His imagination took him the next step onward and, with shocking clarity, showed him the expression of disbelief, anguish, injury, and deep hurt come into her eyes when he told her about Patches and himself.

What was he going to tell her? How was he going to make her understand? Back in Glasgow yesterday, in his agony and fear of losing Patches forever, in the confusion of his mind that came from the realization of what she meant to him, he had seen himself in a way making up to Patches for the things he had not said to her by saying them to Catharine.

His thought had been that Catharine would understand then, that she would not want him when she heard from him the story of his love for Patches. And on the long, drumming flight across the ocean he had even made up the words.

'It's like nothing that ever happened before to me. I've got to tell you, Catharine, so you'll understand. She's part of me.

She's under my skin and in my heart. She's my pain and my delight and my breath. She's in my mind and in my blood wherever I go, whatever I do. I never understood what love was before I knew Patches. There's nothing of me left, nothing that doesn't belong to her and always will. . . .'

Standing at the sideboard, the telephone within his reach, the dark instrument that had so nearly contained the voice of Catharine, Jerry suddenly found himself so filled with shame, horror, and revulsion that he could hardly bear to contemplate it. He thought his knees would give way, and he slumped into a chair and buried his face in his hands. Dreadful lightnings of truth were searing the dark abyss that had opened up before him.

For now that he was home – here in his father's house, where he had been raised, where he had spent his childhood and his boyhood, where he had been taught the creed and tenets of a gentleman – now that for the first time he had begun to think, he knew that the idea that had driven him to take the crazy ride with Eagles was utterly fantastic and completely impossible.

It was the purest madness to have thought that he could walk coolly into Catharine's house, jilt her, win his release, and fly back to his Patches. Life wasn't like that.

Had he really contemplated facing this girl he had known and worshipped for all of his adolescent life, to whom he was engaged by public announcement, who by now had his most recent letter, in which he had written to hint of the close approach of the day when they might be married, to ask her sympathy and understanding because he had fallen in love with someone else? Had he actually thought he could make a love declaration to Catharine about another girl?

The shock of the total collapse of this ridiculous, wholly

illusory boy's world shook him physically and made him feel sick.

Harman Wright got up and came over to his son and put his hand on his shoulder, for he thought the battle won, that his arguments had prevailed, as he had known they would. But he was too wise to press his advantage before he was certain. He was deeply moved by Jerry's trouble, for it brought back things he was quite certain had been long forgotten, and they seemed to vibrate again with Jerry's hurt.

He said: 'Take it easy, son. It's never really as bad as it seems. . . .'

Then he said quietly: 'Look here, Jerry. You haven't thought it out to the end yet. You can't accomplish anything in a rush this way. Go upstairs and take a rest. Don't try to see Catharine tonight. Nobody knows you've been here. Nobody need know. Go back to England and finish your tour of duty. Don't do anything foolish. I know you won't. Then come home to us and see how you feel. How about it? I'll drive you to the airport tonight, and nobody will be any the wiser.' Then he added. 'I know it would make your mother very happy.'

The old rebellion surged in Jerry again. Make his mother happy. Make Catharine happy. . . . Make everybody happy but Patches and himself. . . . And yet the strands of his old life, the Jerry he had been, were beginning to enmesh him, binding him, pulling at him, attaching their tenuous threads to his mind.

Of one thing he was certain. He could not go through with going over to Catharine then and there and breaking the engagement. It was too black a thing to do to add to the burdens of his mind and the weight upon his spirit. But he did want desperately to be alone, to try to think, to regain his sense of values.

He said: 'Okay, Dad. I . . . I can't see Cat now. I'll go up-stairs for a while.' He added: 'Do you think I ought to go see Mother?'

'If you think you're ready to tell her that you're going to go back and wait until –'

Jerry said: 'I'll see her later. . . .' He got up and went out of the room, and Harman heard his slow, heavy footsteps going up the stairs, followed by the scrabbling of Skipper going up with him, stairs his father remembered Jerry never used to go up less than two at a time, and his heart was heavy for him. He was a man who above all wanted to do what was right for those he loved, and there was no doubt in his mind as to what was right.

Things like that happened to kids, and they had to go through them and get over them in their own way – there was nothing you could really do to help, and they hurt like hell while they were going on. But he knew that in the years to come, when Jerry and Catharine would be married and have a home and children of their own, his son would be happy and grateful, and if he remembered the girl in England at all, it would be with the dim recollection of something wonderful that had happened to him when he was young, and not to be regretted.

Harman Wright went to the side table and poured himself a drink, and was startled to find with what clarity of detail he was suddenly thinking of Adrienne and the gay, high-ceilinged, rococo room in the hotel at Mentone, the bald-headed waiter who looked like a gnome, the moon on the sea, the old-fashioned brocaded bell-pull, Adrienne's laugh.

She was so ridiculously gay and sunny, her eyes crinkled at the corners, the ends of her mouth turned up even when her face was in repose. She . . . Harman set his glass down untouched, arose, and went upstairs swiftly to his wife's room to see how she was and bring her encouragement.

Familiar things surrounded Jerry again. His room was exactly as he had left it, the purple-and-white Williams blanket neatly folded over the foot of the bed, the West Point and Westbury High School pennants on the wall next to the framed picture of the championship Westbury football team, taken in his senior year, and on his bureau stood the large framed portrait photograph of Catharine, picking him up with her eyes as it always did when he came into the room, eyes that even in the picture showed the sweetness and clarity of spirit behind them. The photograph shook him, because he had forgotten it was there.

He went to his wardrobe and opened the door and stood there for a moment in a kind of bewilderment looking at his youth. His civilian clothes hung there neatly pressed and brushed as though waiting for him to step into them, and on the shelf above he saw his ice skates and three fielders' mitts, including the first one he had ever had, and which he had outgrown. Standing in a corner were his golf clubs, three tennis rackets in presses, a baseball bat, a fly rod in a case, and his old single-shot .22 rifle. On the floor were some discoloured tennis balls and a deflated football.

He glanced at his books lining the shelves along the wall, from Henty and Alger and the Frank Merriwell series to Scott and Dumas and Conan Doyle, and the set of G. K. Chesterton that Catharine had given him one Christmas. Without knowing he was doing it, he took out a book, held it in his hand for a moment, and then put it back again.

His desk invited him, and he sat down at it and idly pulled open a drawer. It seemed only yesterday that he had been sitting there. He fingered some of the contents. There was his high-school diploma, a half-empty box of cartridges, three golf balls, and the silver medal he had won at the last scholastic track meet. He found an old tasselled dance programme from a club dance when he was fourteen, and, opening it, read the name of 'Catharine', inscribed in his round and then unformed hand seven times. There were letters and an old copy book, a dozen marbles and a set of drawings for putting together a model air-plane, a broken fountain pen and a little packet of tissue paper that he knew contained a lock of Catharine's hair.

Jerry was conscious of the feeling that Catharine's steady, friendly gaze was on him from the photograph, and he closed the drawer with a bang, got up, and laid the picture face down upon the bureau. But almost immediately he went back and stood it up again. He said: 'I've got to stop acting like a kid! . . .'

He took out a crumpled pack of cigarettes and lit one, and thought again of his father and the story he had told him, and it saddened him beyond measure. His young mind fought with a certain kind of stubborn valiance against the destruction of a long-cherished illusion, and he went over his father's phrases, the things he had said, one by one.

And as he did so, aided by his desire to excuse him, certain sentences and ideas lingered, and he found his anger fading. He remembered his father had said:' 'I loved your mother dearly, and I always will. We've had a wonderful life together, and I wouldn't exchange it for any other.'

Jerry thought now that perhaps he better understood his father and what he had been trying to tell him, for the evidence was all about him and had been for all of his life.

It was to be found in the house with its quiet good taste and harmony, the possessions that surrounded them, their friends, the atmosphere that had been made for him into which to be born and educated into manhood, in the kind of person he himself was, the way he thought and acted.

It was, he appreciated, a question of standards. True, they had all been there, ready-made and provided for him until he had made them his habits, but this did not alter their power to hold him, or blind him to the fact that never in his life had he thought of appealing from them. They suited him. He had felt secure and extraordinarily happy in his family life, and believed beyond any doubt, up to that point, that these standards had been a part of his father's success as a husband, parent, provider, and human being. He came back again to that feeling of rightness he had about his family.

His father had only been trying to say to him: 'This is your world, Jerry. You were born and bred into it; it fits you. You'll be happy in it and no other, no matter what you may think or feel now. We've made everything so right for you in every way....'

In a way he felt refreshed and relieved, because he could not bear to be angry with his father. As a boy he had made him a hero for what he was and the things he could do as an athlete. Growing up, he admired and loved him for his kindness and his qualities. He even aimed to follow his footsteps in business and banking. If Jerry had thought much as a boy about what his life would be like when he was grown to manhood, it was always a kind of perpetuation of his own home and the example set therein, an extension of his parents' life and way of living. When the war came it had merely been a postponement.

Now Jerry recalled why he had wanted to be alone, why he had really come to his room. It had been in order to be with Patches again, to be alone with her and near her. And it was with a shock and a feeling of sheer panic that he was aware suddenly that he could not find her.

It was not that she was gone but that momentarily a door seemed to have closed and through it the music of Patches sounded more faintly. It was like looking for someone in a mist, hearing a voice but not being able to see. And Jerry thought of the night in Scotland when they were lost in the storm at the foot of Ben Venue in the Trossachs and she had been silent for so long that he had become alarmed and had groped for her in the dark.

But he was remembering now, and he felt the helpless clinging of her chilled and rain-soaked form, the trusting, beseeching insinuation of her body to his, and the message it told with its surrender that she was sick and in trouble and speechless with cold, and could not tell him otherwise that she needed him.

He was back once more in the yesterday in the rough, low room of the Highland farm-house, where he had crouched before the flickering peat-smoke fire through the night with Patches in his arms, warming her with his heart and never knowing how much he loved her.

Jerry was fearful again, because the cherished picture was fading like a dream that is as vivid as life upon the waking and an hour later has begun to dissolve like summer fog when the sun rises. He could remember the fire but not the fireplace, the smoke-blackened, steaming kettle but not the iron from which it hung, the texture of the blankets wrapping the still form of Patches but not the colour, the sleepy smile at the corner of Patches' mouth but not the mouth itself.

It had seemed then that the shadowy walls of the low, rough chamber leaping in the firelight were the compass of the world. Yesterday was buried and forgotten; Patches was breathing in his arms, and there was no tomorrow. But this was today, and only fragments remained.

From the bureau in his boyhood room the grave, trusting eyes of Catharine Quentin looked down at him. The sweet, well-remembered tones of the hall clock on the stairs chimed the hour of nine, and he listened almost as though he expected to hear his mother's voice call: 'Bedtime, Jerry', as she had when he had been a child. He could smell the summer's night fragrance of the flowers from the garden and hear the familiar voices of kids shouting and playing in the street, music from a radio, and the distant rolling of a train on the Long Island Railroad.

He was home, and England was aeons away and a dream. Gedsborough Airbase in the chill grey of the yet unborn morning – himself sitting high in the nose of his ship with Sam Bognano while the engines thundered in the warm-up and the cavalcade of Liberators began their slow march along the side of the field to the take-off like ghostly elephants – was but a fabric.

The chunk-chunk of the slot machine in the officers' club; Lester Harrison and his mocking eyes; jeep rides down narrow English lanes; London concealing its gutted, broken heart behind the blank façades of still untoppled walls; dreary, hopeless, friendly Kenwoulton and the smell of weary bodies and poverty inside the cinema; the dark shuffling of unseen feet through the steel-and-stone caverns of blacked-out railway stations; the sharp pungency of soft-coal smoke, the impatient, frustrated, falsetto shrieks of the locomotive whistles; and – Patches, Patches, where was she?

He tried to see her in the darkened plotting-room in the operations H.Q. of the Spitfire fighter base where she was stationed, her small head, with the soft bun of brown hair coiled at the back, bent over the crisscross squares of the radar screen, rigid with concentration as the light beam swept about the dial on its eternal circle, picking up the momentary glows, the fleeting luminosities that indicated the spot where there was an aircraft in the sky.

Jerry thought of himself sending out thoughts of Patches like the radar waves, and trying to catch upon the panel of his mind the tiny bright reflections of her being. Then he glanced at his watch and made the calculation of the difference in time and realized that Patches would not be at ops. It was not quite morning yet in England. She would still be in bed in her room on the upper floor of the dingy house in Bishop's Lane, sleeping.

And now he could see her, for he remembered her sleeping, the sweet and touching innocence of it, the little hollow spot at her temple and the curve of her cheek, the brown lashes against the clear white skin, the thick coil of silken hair down one shoulder, and the way she kept one hand curled beneath her chin. She slept with all the warmth and softness of a kitten.

The door was open again, and relief at finding Patches mingled with the loneliness and heartache that came from the reliving of moments with her, awakenings of yearning for her presence that only served to throw into relief the realization that he had solved nothing. Nothing was certain beyond the fact that in less than four hours he would be back again at La Guardia Airport to board ship and fly back to England and whatever awaited him there.

What did await him there? Sweating out the remainder of his missions, briefing, take-off, flight, flak and fear, battle, and the racking struggle homeward with battle damage, or the joy and relief that came from a pushover assignment, interrogation, mess, movie, boredom, sleep, the routine of the air war. . . .

What would happen between Patches and him? Would they

148

take up where they had left off, would there be stolen moments of intimacy together in some grubby room, where he would try to recapture the high romance of the honeymoon in the Paradise of the Highlands, or would they dance as usual, and sit at their table as though nothing had ever happened between them, to part with a casual good night at the clubhouse door when the lorries came at midnight to take the girls back to town?

There seemed to be two of Patches now: the quiet, undistinguished little mouse who had been his companion to pass the hours at the Saturday-night dances or of an evening in Kenwoulton, just another British girl in the light-blue uniform of the RAF to whom, between the times they happen to be together, he never gave so much as a passing thought, and that other Patches to whom he was indissolubly wedded.

And as he thought of her, fears and doubts once more entered Jerry's mind. Supposing it hadn't meant as much to Patches as it had to him? What if he offered himself to her, asked her to marry him in spite of everything, and she rejected him? There might even have been someone for whom she cared, off with the British armies or at sea. Her going away with him might have been on an impulse, a momentary escape from reality and wartime strain. And when he struggled against the torture of the thought, he would hear the cynical, brittle voice of Major Lester Harrison, the man who had been his model and who knew all about such things – 'This isn't the U.S.A. Girls aren't as puritanical as they are back home.'

He tried to remember how she had looked and what she had done when he had told her that Saturday night, so many ages ago at the dance, about being engaged to marry a girl back home, and that it had to be understood that there wasn't to be anything serious between him and Patches, and that everything between them was to be over when they returned from Scotland, and he could not recall her face or her expression.

But he did remember her saying: 'I shan't change my mind. It will be beautiful. And when it's over, we'll shake hands and say good-bye....'

And that's how it had happened later.... Later? Yesterday! Never a sign, never a tear, not so much as a trembling of her fingers when the slowly accelerating London-bound express had broken the casual farewell grip of their hands. 'Good-bye, Patches...' and only her cool 'God bless, Jerry....'

That was how he had read the rules of the game. That was how Patches had played it. It was he who was acting like a mooning, lovesick kid, crying for something that was over and done with. And he had wanted to be a man! Then why in God's name didn't he learn how to act like one?...

The turmoil within brought him to his feet in a kind of desperation and took him to the window of his room, where he stood looking out over the short gravel driveway and the deep green of the shade trees under the glow of the lamps of the entrance gate.

Diagonally across the street, half-hidden behind elms, lay the warm, friendly mass of light and shadows that was Catharine's house. He could see the white shingles illuminated softly by beams from the upper story, and there was light from the french windows of the drawing-room, where the lamps were lit. He knew the house, inside and out, as well as his own.

Jerry gazed at the house across the street. Catharine was there. She moved behind those walls somewhere in calm serenity and utter faith in him. He remembered how she had looked late that afternoon when he had seen her on the street in front of the library, and her figure came alive in his mind with a kind of painful clarity.

A half a hundred yards, a street that could be crossed in a few strides to come from darkness into light. England suddenly became as distant and remote as the farthest planet. He thought about Catharine and himself and the long, sweet, peaceful years they had known each other. . . .

3

LONELY and depressing as it was to be back in Kenwoulton
quartered in the dank and gloomy house in Bishop's Lane,
Patches was in a way glad that she had come home first and by
herself. It would be several days before Jerry returned, and she
was grateful for the respite it gave her to collect herself, to
think a little, to try to bring to an end the war between her
mind and her emotions.

She had arrived in the late afternoon, and there was nobody
in the house when she went up to her room. She did not pause
at the foot of the stairs, where the wonderful hegira with Jerry
had begun. '. . . at thirty-one minutes past ten hours, the morning of 18 June' – their voyage together had ended in the train in
St Enoch's Station in Glasgow. It was when the railway carriage
in which she had been standing so straight and tearless at the
window had reached the first bend at the end of the platform,
and she lost sight of the diminishing figure of the boy with the
dark hair who was holding his crumpled, rakish soldier's cap on
high, that Patches looked down at her watch and, shielded by
the rising clatter of the wheels, whispered: '. . . and it ended at
one minute past nine, on 27 June, for ever,' and the first bright
drops had fallen upon her wrist and splashed from the dial of
her watch.

When she arrived at Kenwoulton, Patches had hurried home
and to her room to change her clothes. There was a kind of
urgency upon her to lay aside the civilian garments and return
to the stiff, dowdy anonymity of her uniform, as though by

shedding the apparel of one life and assuming the garb of another she could leave behind all the memories, the longings, and the heartaches.

Embraced by the familiar cloth of the Air Force skirt and tunic, she felt almost at ease, sheltered, and protected, and her heart lifted. It was not difficult the next day to go back to her duties and her old way of life, to slip into familiar routines of work and concentration that occupied her mind to lull her into a sense of false security. But soon she was to know that there was no escape from herself or from Jerry.

For Kenwoulton was full of Jerrys, American flyers who, even though they did not look like Jerry, reminded her of him, with their trim battle jackets, silver wings, and rows of stars and ribbons, their clear, bold, mischievous eyes, the expressions of their mouths, their careless gait, and, above all, their voices and speech, as though cut from a pattern.

These were but externals, but Patches found herself looking for Jerry among them. Her eyes followed their figures, the set of their shoulders, the freedom of their carriage, and she found herself yearning to be with them, to hear them talk, because it would bring her nearer to Jerry, and it came as a shock to her to find how great this longing was and that nothing apparently had changed in her.

But many things had changed in her, and this was yet a greater shock when she encountered herself in the mirror. It was the first time she had paused to look at Patches. It was another girl who gazed back at her, and she was frightened.

With whose eyes was she looking at the face and form in the glass, and whose eyes were staring back? It was she, and yet she saw and felt subtle differences, changes in bearing, expression, and personality of which she had not been aware. Something of her that was familiar seemed lost, something new that was strange appeared to have been added. It was with a dreadful and growing feeling of loneliness that she studied her own form and features in the mirror. Jerry was gone for ever. But what if the Patches she knew, and with whom she had lived in a kind of inner peace and contentment, were gone too?

She blamed only herself for what she was suffering and for the more intense suffering she knew was to follow. She had done something that she felt in her heart was right but that she knew in her conscience was wrong. She had gone away deliberately with a boy who was engaged to another girl, who had told her that in the end he would go home and marry this girl. She had gone into it with her eyes open. Jerry had never told Patches that he loved her. He had made the nature of the affair plain from the beginning.

Patches was far too honest to make excuses for herself. Her love for Jerry, the depth and power of the emotion, had come to be so much a part of her that she did not even think of it as a compelling reason for what she had done. She knew that she and Jerry and Jerry's girl at home, people everywhere, were living in a world that was going through a terrible convulsion that affected the lives of everyone.

She knew too that she lived at the battlefront, where living or dying was a daily accident, and that day after day this boy she had grown to love above all else in the world flew away to combat from which he might never come back. The line, 'Three of our aircraft failed to return,' had become a part of her habit of living and thinking, for she too was connected intimately with the hazards of an airbase. Week after week, boys with whom she laughed or joked, or even went out with for an evening, vanished from the roster, until the ritual of grief itself became superficial. Menaced by bombs and rockets, the incident of one's own living and breathing and being was reduced to a matter of luck. One did not want to die, but the chance was ever present, and therefore one lived more sharply, breathed more deeply, caressed the earth more firmly with one's feet, looked with a more tender and loving eye upon the spring, green grass, a sunny day, children playing in the street. ...

But sitting alone in her room in the early evening the day after her return, Patches refused to admit these thoughts in extenuation of what she had done. Her punishment for her transgression had already begun. It would soon become more severe. For Jerry would be coming back shortly. He would be near by, at Gedsborough. He would be coming in to Kenwoulton. She might meet him on the street, pass him, or encounter him close by in one of the little groups of flyers always wandering about.

It was his nearness or the accidents of encounter that Patches knew she would dread. She had already made up her mind that when he returned she would not see him again. A chapter in her life was closed. She could no longer attend the dances on Saturday night at the officers' club at Gedsborough, or go to the pictures with him, or spend one of their gay, crazy evenings of pub-crawling. For she knew she did not have the strength to see him or be with him and conceal her love for him.

Downstairs the telephone rang, and Patches noticed how automatically she sharpened her listening, how the old habits and hopes reasserted themselves. This was the hour when Jerry usually called, and she remembered how in the old days she always hoped it would be he who called first rather than one of the other boys from the Spitfire airbase with whom she sometimes had dates.

She heard the high-pitched giggle of one of the other girls speaking on the telephone from below, and disconnected her senses from the sounds as she looked about her room with a kind of desperation and harrowing unease. Her favourite books

155

stood on the shelf by the window, but she did not have the courage to open one. There were photographs of her father and mother looking down at her from their accustomed place on her chiffonier, and Patches thought that she did not even have a picture of Jerry, not so much as a pair of silver wings or a shoulder patch, to remember him by. And with a kind of bitter despair that brought even the shadow of a smile to her mouth, she realized the inadequacy of objects and at the same time the superfluousness of anything needed to remind her of Jerry. . . .

She had not known. She had not dreamed what it would do to her, even after the inner struggle that had preceded her so blithely going off with him that June morning.

Jerry was the first boy Patches had truly loved; he was the first man to whom she had given herself. She had made this gift out of love and generosity and the unstilled hunger of youth for youth – the yearning of love that needs an answering love to hush its cries – but she could not in truth have known or suspected what would happen to her because of the giving, the changes that were to be wrought upon her.

She had thought to snatch a moment of happiness in a crumbling world, to give one brief instant of existence to her love for Jerry before she put him forever out of her life. She had known she would not forget him, that he would always be a sweet and tender memory, but she had counted upon time to help dim the dreams she had made around him. She had not foreseen what she now knew, that there was no longer anything in life but Jerry.

She belonged to Jerry, everything that she was – her conscious thoughts, her person, her mind, her heart, the deep, swelling buds of womanhood, that were bursting within her – awake, asleep, living, dying, breathing, walking, wherever she might be, to the ends of time, she belonged to him. He possessed her, and it was this knowledge of his possession of her that brought such a terror and trembling to her heart. Nothing was left of her to be recovered. She was utterly and hopelessly lost.

There was now not even, as she had hoped, any refuge to be found in memories. For during the days that they had lived together and grown closer to each other, Jerry had come to be her husband in every sense. All the many attentions and courtesies and protections with which a man surrounds a woman had been hers. Kindnesses, tenderness, little thoughtful acts of his that grew out of their living together, came to be unbearable to Patches as memories because they mirrored the perfection of their brief and total happiness. It was like the first time that Jerry had registered at the hotel in Invesnaid: 'Lieutenant and Mrs Gerald Wright,' and Patches could not bear to look while he did it. Now there was nothing but pain when she remembered the days and the nights when she had lived with Jerry, passing as his wife.

She fought the past by trying to plan the future, and thought about what she would do if and when Jerry telephoned her. She remembered his smile in the station and his confident 'See you when I get back to Kenwoulton. . . .' The trip had indeed been nothing more than an episode to him, to be continued thereafter on the careless footing of friendship. She was not angry with him for this. He had never lied to her. But she wondered whether she would have the strength to deny him, when he called, to say: 'I'm sorry, Jerry, but it's best if we don't see one another any more,' or to refuse to speak to him at all, to make the break clean and sharp.

And yet she so longed to see him once more. The desire manifested itself in the fantasies she threw up against such denial, that Jerry had done nothing to deserve such treatment, that it would be kinder to see him once more, to remind him of the terms of their friendship and to point out that it was best for both to stand by those terms. And while she was with him again for that last meeting, she could possess him once more with her eyes, see his smile, and hear his laugh, touch his hand, study again the strong angle of his jaw and the shape and colour of his eyes that so touched her heart. She would memorize every dear line of his features and inflection of his voice. ... Patches realized that the telephone was ringing again and that she was listening.

She covered her ears with her hands for a moment, so shocked and desperate was she at her own weakness. It was over, over, over! She had no right to think thoughts of seeing him again. She at once resolved that when he returned and called her, she would be out, or busy. There would be – there must be – a clean break. She called upon all the inner strength and dignity that had carried her through life and the bitter difficult war years, and promised herself this. Her head came up, she breathed deeply, her whole body stiffened with resolve.

'Coeeee, Patches! Are you there?' It was one of the girls calling from below. Patches went to the door and answered. The girl said: 'Telephone. It's for you. ...'

Jerry! Perhaps he was calling her from Scotland. He might even have cut short his leave and come home. All resolves and promises and steeling of herself against this moment were gone. To hear his voice once more, his gay careless, infectious greeting: 'Hi, Patches, what's cooking?' She raced down the stairs breathlessly, in panic, lest something should happen to the connexion to break the slender strand that for the moment would bind her to Jerry again.

She picked up the receiver. 'Hello, this is Patches. ...'

There was a moment of silence in the telephone while every

fibre of her vibrated with the expectancy of hearing Jerry's voice; in her mind she was already hearing it, and her heart was framing her reply, preparing the softness and tenderness in her voice. . . .

'Hello, hello. . . . I say, Patches, you're back, aren't you? That's jolly good. What about a turn at the flicks tonight?'

Patches thought she would die from disappointment. It wasn't Jerry. She knew the voice, but for the moment could not even think who it was.

'Hello, hello? I say, are you there, Patches? This is Allan.'

She knew now and said faintly: 'Hello, Allan.' It was one of the RAF pilots, Allan Peters, from the nearby Spitfire base where Patches worked as a radar technician in operational headquarters. He was a nice and rather innocuous boy with whom she had had occasional dates in the past.

He was saying: 'There's a new flick with Lana Turner at the Kensington. I thought we might pop over. . . .'

'I . . . I don't know, Allan. . . .' Patches was sick with disappointment and with shame at her own weakness. What had happened to her determination to break off with Jerry? At the first slender hope of hearing his voice she had come rushing to the telephone.

'Quite all right, Patches. I just thought if you weren't doing anything . . .'

Patches did not want to see Allan or go to the pictures. She could not bear the thought of being with anyone; she did not even wish to leave her room and the safety of its walls and familiar objects. And then the reaction to her own weakness set in. She had always gone with Allan before when he had asked her. Somewhere life must begin again, somehow the old threads be picked up. But it was more to punish herself for having given in to her longing for Jerry so quickly that she said: 'All right, Allan, I'll go with you.'

'Right-o, Patches. I'll be around for you at the usual. Cheerio. . . .'

Allan Peters called for Patches, and they saw the picture at the Kensington and then went for some fish and chips and sat in a booth, where Allan found himself studying Patches with a kind of puzzled interest. He was of the breed – pink-cheeked, with curly sand-coloured hair, weak chin and weak mouth, over which he had raised an edge of RAF moustache – one of those boys who looked footling, silly, and rather useless and who was a holy terror in a Spitfire in combat.

Allan had known Patches for some time as a girl who was pleasant to talk to, or take for a walk in the country, or have as a neighbour in a movie theatre. But he had never been aware of her in any sense as a girl who might be desirable. Now he found himself unable to take his pale eyes from her face. Something about her that he did not understand, that he had never noticed before, was stirring him queerly, making him uneasy and yet excited. He sat more closely to her and sometimes carelessly let his hand rest upon the table so that it touched hers. And he kept searching her face, and once when she bent her head to his proffered cigarette-lighter, he quickly breathed in the fragrance from her hair.

He inquired about how she had spent her leave, and when she satisfied him with generalities, he said suddenly: 'I say, Patches, what's come over you? Do you know you've changed a lot since the last time we were together?'

'Changed, Allan? What do you mean?' She turned her eyes on him, eyes that were wide with alarm, though he did not interpret the look since he could not know of the panic his confirmation of her fears inspired in her. For a moment Patches

160

had the terrible sensation of being stripped naked and bound hand and foot in the market place to be stared at. Dear God, could everyone now see?

'Oh, I don't know. I mean you're quite different, you know. Almost as though you. ... I say, Patches, would you mind very much if I kissed you?'

Patches was feeling sick and dizzy inside and did not know what to do or say. 'He knows ... he can tell ... he feels it ...' was going through her mind. This was a part of what was to be from now on, the things she had brought upon herself, things she would be called upon to face. Allan reached over and kissed her awkwardly on the side of the head and took her hand in his. He said huskily: 'Damn it all, Patches! Am I going to fall in love with you?'

Patches murmured: 'Don't fall in love with me, Allan,' but did not have the strength or the fight to disengage her hand from his.

But it was on the way home in the dark alley of Bishop's Lane that Allan suddenly said her name, 'Patches', and turned and took her in his arms, pressing his mouth on hers, keeping it there, holding her imprisoned by the desire of his body.

She did not resist. She let it happen as a punishment to herself. It took all of her courage, but she spared herself nothing. She felt the warmth and rapidity of his breathing, and, in the wan light of the semi-blacked-out street lamp, saw the moist glitter of his eyes, and in the horrible, endless moment of the embrace she came to know the meaning of hell on earth.

He relaxed his hold for a moment to look at her, his throat working, his face pale; then his hands were reaching for her again, crying hoarsely: 'Patches. ... I say, Patches, I ...'

But she was running now, running as fast as she could through the street, her feet barely touching the curved cobblestones, running and sobbing, with the darkness all through her, inside as well as outside, as though she were a part of the heavy blackness that would never know the light again. She heard him cry her name once more, and the heavier drumming of the footsteps on the pavement, before she reached the house and safety inside.

She ran up the stairs to her room, where she locked the door and then threw herself on to her bed and cried terribly for Jerry. Her crying was the miserable, hopeless weeping of the abandoned, of the woman denied the protection of her man.

She spoke his name, calling upon him again and again and again: 'Oh Jerry, Jerry ... Jerry!' Why wasn't he there to shield her? If he loved her, he would be there with her, and nothing could happen to her. Into her crying crept the hysteria of the fear that had been with her ever since she had come back, when she had known that her security was gone, her safety assailed, her citadel destroyed. Allan had read it on her that she was now prey to all men. There was no one to whom she could turn.

Her crying now was like that of a fear-stricken child calling wildly in the darkness. She beat on the mattress with her fists and called: 'Jer-*reeeee*, Jer-*eeeeee*! Please, Jerry. ...' She cried for him to come before it was too late and take her out of the darkness that was engulfing her. 'Oh, please, Jer-*reeeee*! ...'

The lights in the house on the other side of Severn Avenue exercised a kind of compulsion upon Jerry as he stood by the window of his room and stared across the quiet, deserted street, letting his thoughts wander where his feet would not go, across the few yards separating the two Long Island homes.

He had been standing there thinking for a long time. The hour was past eleven. Through the summer-green curtain of trees he had seen the lights in Catharine's house shift from the ground floor to the upper storey. Soon they would blink out, and then he would feel rather than see the dark mass as he had all through his boyhood.

It was there, with its white-painted shingle sides and dark, slanting roof with the square, flower-bordered balcony over the conservatory with the New England wing featuring the huge studio window opening out from the end on to the bordered brick walk. For the moment it was inescapable. It was as firmly implanted in his mind as it was affixed to its foundations. He knew every beam and stone in it as he knew his own. It had acquired a living personality through having sheltered Catharine, and, through her, his hopes for so long. He had lived and grown with this house from the day, so many years ago, that the Quentins had moved there.

It was there he had gone to play, first as a child, later as an adolescent. Inside those walls he had attended Catharine's first birthday party after her arrival. From that day on, a glamour had settled upon the house that had never been dispelled.

Jerry remembered Catharine on her seventh birthday – he had been eight – and how she had looked in her blue organdie dress, puffed at the shoulders so that she seemed like a winged angel. Her shining hair hung down to her waist and was tied with a big blue bow.

These were the pictures, recollections, and sensations that filled his mind now with startling clarity and vividness, and he felt again something of the thrill and sweetness of that day when he had experienced the first faint tap of manhood upon his shoulders, and the world was filled with lovely creatures, all pink and blue and white and scented with silken hair and starched ribbons and soft dresses, candlelight and games and good things to eat, and above all the fairy presence of the dearest and most enchanting of them all – Catharine.

There had been a new and wholly unforgettable emotion encountered when, with the almost imperceptible yet unmistakable signals of childhood, Catharine had singled him out as her favourite at the party. With a shy glance, or a momentary return to the present he had brought her, or in the way in which she manoeuvred when sides were drawn for the games, she managed to let him know she liked him best and wanted him near her.

For days afterwards Jerry had walked on air. He lived and dreamed on Catharine's radiance and the bright, rosy memories of each crowded minute he had spent in her presence. Day and night were devoted to the rearing of glorious battlements in the sky and the rescuing of Catharine in fantasy from magnificently invented and horrible dangers. He dwelt upon the time when he would grow up and marry her, and saw her always at his side, unchanged in her blue dress with the angel-wing sleeves, her heavy, gleaming hair swinging, as she moved her head, or brushing softly against his face or hand.

During the long years of his journey from childhood to adolescence there had been other interests, and girls had drifted temporarily into the background, but even in that period when, outwardly, girls were beneath his notice, he would sometimes in his mind steal back to the day of the party and recapture the glow and the sweet dizziness that had beset him. And always her house was standing there so comfortably across the street. He saw it every day as he went to school and came home.

The memories persisted. Jerry could not bar them from his mind, because every object that surrounded him, even the light and shadow of the gentle night, was a part of them. He was home; he was doubly home, and the spirit and the presence of

Catharine were something living, beckoning across the tiny gulf of the asphalt street, calling him with a thousand voices to which he could not close his ears. It was on just such a summer's night as this in Westbury, when the elm leaves were rustled into changing their shadowy patterns on the ground by a cool breeze from the ocean side, and there had been soft starlight, distant music, and distant laughter, that he had first dared to kiss her.

He was seventeen then. She had not kissed him back, but, after a moment of silence, had got up from the swing on the porch and gone into the house, and he knew that he had offended her. He remembered the hell through which he had gone, how he felt that he had placed himself beyond the pale by offering her a mortal insult, and had tortured himself until she forgave him and they had made up.

Rooted there by the window in his room, Jerry found himself reliving, step by step, emotion by emotion, his romance with the girl across the way, until it seemed more and more fantastic that he should be there and she so near to him, separated only by the width of the darkened street.

But for all the memories, the yesterday still ached powerfully in his heart, and Jerry found himself confused and baffled by the presence of the two emotions. For Patches, even though he could not see her clearly, was not so much a memory as someone who had come to live within him and whose absence created a void that nothing could fill.

It was this recollection of the feeling that a union had taken place between them – something beautiful, strong, harmonious, and indissoluble – that turned his disturbed mind to summoning her again, if only she would come. Why was it he could not place Patches beyond the misery and dulled yearning that permeated him? Why were there only fragments of her to be snatched at – the straight line of her back, the tender slope of

165

her shoulders, the way her eyes would steal a look at him when she thought he wasn't watching, her little skip when she was happy, or perhaps no more than the deep breath she drew in before she began to tell something important – when every detail of Catharine was as clear as though she were standing there in the room beside him?

Could it be true, as his father had intimated, that in the end he would never regret marrying Catharine, and that as he grew older, lived and prospered amongst his own people and his family, the strains of Patches would become fainter and fainter and in the end die away, that he might some day speak of her as his father had of Adrienne?

Jerry went over to his desk and opened a drawer, searching for a moment until he found what he sought – a newspaper clipping, with a picture of Catharine, announcing their engagement. It was the same photograph of her that stood on his bureau, and her clear, level gaze was upon him as he reread the short paragraph:

Mr and Mrs Frederic Quentin, of No. 15 Severn Avenue, Westlake Park, Long Island, announce the engagement of their daughter Miss Catharine Rowland Quentin, to U.S. Army Air Forces 2nd Lieutenant Gerald H. Wright, son of Mr and Mrs Harman Wright, of No. 12 Severn Avenue, Westlake Park. Miss Quentin attended Rosemary Hall and the Seton School, of Noroton, Conn. She is a member of the New York Junior League and is prominent in Red Cross and blood-donor work in Westbury. Before enlisting in the Air Forces, Mr Wright graduated from Westbury High School, and was attending Williams College where he was a member of the football and track teams, the Ionian Club, and the Alpha Delta Phi Fraternity. He is leaving for advanced training at Camp Stickney, Texas.

The small slip of paper Jerry held in his fingers was like a chain that bound him indissolubly to Catharine. He remembered how beautiful and glorious and right the world had seemed the day it was published. Now it haunted him. Everyone had seen it, had read that he and Catharine were promised to each other, had looked upon her picture. It had happened. It could not be erased. . . .

The pain of Patches was a misty longing, as though a grey veil had descended between them. She was there. He could feel her presence, but he could not reach her. And confronting him was the visible, public proof of what had once been his heart's desire. He stood there, wearily looking at the clipping, no longer seeing the type, and not knowing what to do. He was too tired to think any more.

Harman Wright was in the library, waiting and smoking quietly when his wife came in. Her eyes were swollen, and she looked like a wraith. The shock of the domestic disaster had really made her ill. She was torn between love for Jerry and love for Catharine, the desire to see and be with him, fear and hope, the disruption of all her plans as well as by the change in Jerry. Harman went to her at once.

'Helen, my dear. . . . You shouldn't have come down. You're –'

'Harman . . . I had to know. Where's Jerry? Has he gone out? Has he gone over to see . . .' She couldn't finish the expression of fear that was so painful to her.

'To see Catharine? No, I don't think so. He went up to his room to think things out. I haven't heard him come down.'

Helen began to cry nervously. 'Harman, I want to go to him. He's my baby. I haven't seen anything of him since he's been home. He needs me. . . .'

Harman Wright said: 'Wait, Helen. Let him be a little longer. He has to work this out by himself.' His eyes went quickly to the wall clock. It was past eleven. Every second that ticked by made it more certain that Jerry would not see Catharine that night. In his heart he felt the danger was over and the victory assured. He was sure that once Jerry got past this hurdle he would come to his senses.

Helen sank into a chair and continued to cry bitterly. 'I'm so afraid, Harman. Jerry's different. Something has happened to him. I can feel it. I'm his mother. We mustn't let him do it, for his own sake. It's only Jerry I'm thinking about now. . . . I don't know what to do. . . .'

Harman said gently: 'He's growing up, Helen. War does that. But he's still our boy. And when he was in trouble he came home to us. Jerry will do what is right. He won't try to see Catharine tonight. When it came to the point where he was leaving to go over there, he realized by himself that he couldn't do it. I had a little talk with him. I told him . . .' he checked himself. 'He knows how much it would hurt you. . . .'

His quiet manner had a soothing effect upon Helen, and made her turn more strongly to him for comfort and reassurance. She cried: 'How could he say he loved this other girl? Catharine was meant for him. We've made everything so right for him, for both of them. It's his whole future. . . .'

Harman said: 'He knows he loves Catharine. Things like the other girl sometimes happen to boys when they're away from home and under the stress of war. When they have the stuff in them that Jerry has, and the right background, they come through.'

He put his arm around his wife's shoulder. 'See here, Helen, buck up. Years from now, when Jerry and Catharine are married and have kids of their own, we'll look back on our carryings on tonight and laugh. . . .'

'Harman . . . promise me. . . .'

Helen was so eager and pathetic in her trust of him that Harman almost smiled. He patted her hand. 'I don't think you need worry too much. I'll promise you that Jerry is a hundred per cent. It's getting late. I'll go upstairs for a moment and see how he's making out. Wait here. . . .'

'You promised, Harman. . . .'

He went up the stairs not quite at ease but hoping strongly that things would come out as he had said. These hopes rose when he knocked on the door of Jerry's room and went in. Jerry was standing by an open desk drawer with a newspaper clipping in his hand. As his father came in he dropped it quickly into the drawer and closed it. Harman had seen that it was his engagement announcement to Catharine, but he wisely refrained from alluding to it. But the very fact that Jerry had got it out. . . .

He said: 'I just thought I'd look in, Jerry, and see how things were. . . .'

'Come in, Dad.' Jerry was glad that there was no longer any anger in his heart against his father. He asked: 'Is it late?'

'Eleven-thirty.' Harman Wright came into the room and sat down on the edge of the bed as he used to when Jerry was a little boy. He lit a cigarette and smoked silently for a moment, waiting for Jerry to speak, but when his son said nothing, he came to the point.

'Have you made up your mind what you think you'll do?'

'Be on that ship when she takes off at two in the morning,' Jerry replied with a kind of grim decisiveness that made his father smile.

'I can see your point.' Harman glanced at his watch again. 'And Catharine? You can hardly –'

Jerry said briefly: 'There's no use in my seeing Cat tonight, the way things have turned out. . . .'

'I think you're being very wise, Jerry. . . .'

Jerry did not feel wise, but it was curious that he could not help feeling good when his father praised him. It had always been that way. He said: 'I don't know about that, sir. I just know I've got to be on that plane if I don't want the book thrown at me. I've done a lot of figuring until I just can't think any more. I've got to go back and I've got twenty more missions, and that's that.' He hesitated, and then went on: 'I'd rather Cat didn't know I'd been here. I'd just like to skip the whole thing –'

He had been about to add: '– for the time being,' but his father interrupted him with a lusty: 'Good boy, Jerry!'

To Harman's wishful mind it was Jerry's final decision as he had hoped for it, and he did not notice the sharp way his son's head came up, or his look. He sprang up from the bed and took him by the arm, leading him towards the door. 'We'll have a drink on that. And your mother will be very, very happy. She's waiting downstairs. . . .'

When they came into the library Helen arose with a little cry: 'Jerry, darling . . .' and came to him.

Moved by her appearance and her unhappiness, Jerry took her in his arms and held her, letting her cry, patting her shoulder tenderly, and saying: 'Aw gee, Mother, don't cry so!'

Harman too stood by, saying: 'Now, Mother. Pull yourself together. It's all right. Everything is all right. Jerry is –'

Helen heard him through her tears and held her son off for a moment, searching his face and then that of her husband to see whether he was telling the truth. 'Jerry, darling . . . Harman . . . are you –'

Harman said: 'Perfectly sure, Helen. Jerry has told me he is going back to England and has decided against doing anything foolish. Everything is quite straightened out and just as it was before. Catherine need never know that Jerry has been home....'

Jerry again looked sharply at his father. It was wrong of him to lie to his mother, even to calm her. He had never known him to do that. And then, with a kind of slowly growing panic, he realized that Harman Wright was not lying. He was perfectly sincere and believed completely in what he was saying.

Before Jerry could speak a word his mother's arms were about him again and she was sobbing her happiness, kissing him, and then leaning her head on his shoulder in the weakness of the relief she felt. She said: 'Oh, Jerry ... you've made me so happy! I just couldn't have borne it otherwise....'

Bewildered, Jerry could only hold his mother, one hand still automatically patting her shoulder. He had never said that he was giving up Patches. He didn't even know in his own mind what he would do or what would happen to him. He had come to no solution of his problem. He had said no more than that he was returning to England to finish his tour of duty without seeing Catharine....

His mother was saying: 'Come sit beside me, Jerry,' and he let her lead him to the low, leather divan, where she held him off and looked at him long and searchingly. She said: 'Jerry, dear, you've made me happy again. I couldn't bear the thought of anything coming between you and Catharine. It destroyed me, Jerry. It kept me from being with you when I wanted to enjoy every second of your stay.'

Jerry stole a quick glance at his father, but there was no hint of trickery in his face. His was the calm, satisfied expression of a man who has ridden out a domestic tempest and seen all his fleet safely into harbour. All was right with *his* world again....

Helen Wright took her son's face between her hands. She was

still emotionally shaken and nearly hysterical with relief. She said: 'Jerry, darling, believe me, I was only thinking of your happiness. You're my baby and everything in the world to me. To see you making a mistake was more than I could bear. You and Catharine were meant for one another from the day you were born. Now that it's all over I can tell you how much it means to your father and to me. . . .'

Jerry was no longer capable of protest or even of thinking. He said lamely: 'I know, Mother,' for he had neither the energy nor the will to contradict her and upset her again.

He could not even know what was in his mind any longer, or be sure of what he wanted. He felt herded and crowded into a blind alley, a corner from which there was no escape. Everything that had happened – his struggles with himself, his surroundings, his physical and mental weariness engendered by lack of sleep, and now the powerful impact of the will and the desires of his father and mother – all combined to weaken and sap his own will so that he was incapable of coordinating his thoughts.

He was startled by the sneeze of the soda siphon. His father was mixing a drink. Helen Wright sniffed, dabbed at her eyes, and said: 'Pour me one too, Harman. I need it,' and then she even achieved a kind of rueful smile as her husband prepared a Scotch and soda and brought it to her. When she took it from him, she leaned her cheek against his hand for a moment and looked up at him like a child for whom someone had fixed a broken toy.

Harman raised his glass and said: 'Here's how, and good luck, son! . . .'

Helen Wright murmured: 'To your safe return, dear. . . .'

Patches said: 'God bless, Jerry. . . .'

It was as though she were standing there in the room as he

had known and loved her. For that one moment every detail of her face and figure was clear. Nothing was missing. Patches had returned.

He saw everything – the hang of her silken blouse about her small wrists, the luminosity of her eyes, their shine and colour, the little shadow smiles and movements at the corners of her mouth, and the soft coils of light-brown hair braided at the sides of her head.

She was all there – the proud, gentle set of her head upon her neck, the slight turn of her chin, the fall of her clothing about her figure, the straight, slim legs ending in flat-heeled shoes. Every tender, loving, meaningful inflection was remembered in her voice when she seemed to speak the familiar toast: 'God bless, Jerry. . . .'

For an instant the room seemed to quiver, to be filled with the illumination of her presence, and then Jerry found himself staring through her, as it were, at his father and mother as they raised their highball glasses to him, and he had the queer and uncomfortable feeling that they were strangers to him and that he was wishing that he were away from them.

He felt more lonely and lost than ever before in his life. For these were people he knew in his heart he really loved, and yet he wished to be quit of them. He knew it was not their fault that he had failed to find in them the sympathy and support, the understanding of his dilemma, that he needed. But because of the clarity of his knowledge that there was no help to be found here, and because the clear, beloved vision of Patches had emphasized his loss, the realization that he did not know to whom to turn or what to do, he wanted now only to escape from their presence, their voices, the house, the room, the objects therein that were strangling him. . . .

Harman Wright looked at his watch and cleared his throat.

173

'I hate to do this, but ... it'll take us about fifty-five minutes ...'

It was like a release, and Jerry was on his feet almost in-
stantly over his mother's protests. He moved automatically
through the farewells, retrieved his cap from the hall closet,
picked up Skipper and ruffled his head and rubbed his nose.
His father asked: 'Did you have a bag, son?' and then shook
his head over a war where one made a three-thousand-mile
jump without so much as a brief-case. Then he thought about
money and said: 'How are you fixed for cash, son? Here, better
let me give you some,' and pressed some bills on Jerry. Reston
appeared momentarily to say good-bye and wish him luck.

Helen put her arms around him and kissed him again and
again with a kind of desperate fervour and said over and over:
'Write often, dear.... Do be careful. ... Remember how we
worry over you here. ... We love you, Jerry. ...'

In the end his father broke it up by saying with something of
the air of a conspirator: 'I've got the car out in back. It will be
less conspicuous to leave by the side driveway. Well. ...'

And then at last Jerry was in the soft, cool darkness, spinning
down the white ribbon of concrete through the tunnel carved
out of the night by the headlights of his father's roadster. He was
so tired by then that he seemed to be drifting from dream to
dream as he listened to his father, who was at the wheel, talking
of plans when the war should be over.

Harman Wright said: 'You may not want to go back to
school when you come back. I guess you've learned a hell of a
lot in the Air Force for that matter. On the other hand, once
you've started, there's nothing quite as weak as half a college
education. A degree is something you'll never regret, but
you'll make up your own mind about that. And for that matter,
there's nothing to prevent you from marrying Catharine when

you come home and then finishing up at Williams. You know that you won't want for anything. There'll probably be a lot of chaps who will do just that. . . .'

The tyres made a fat, whining noise on the road.

Harman went on: 'Do you remember the Owens' house, the little brick one out on Fenimore Road next to the pond, a half-mile down from the turnpike? It's for sale. Your mother and I stopped in last week and looked at it. It's in perfect condition.'

Jerry saw himself standing outside the Owens' brick house down by the pond, looking at it, but he could not go inside or see anything but the door and the white shutters on the windows.

Harman said casually: 'I dropped in on Griggs, the agent, and had a little talk with him. It would be ideal for you two. . . .'

His father continued to rattle on with plans for his future through a ride that to Jerry seemed dizzying, unreal, and interminable, until at last the weaving searchlight beacon of La Guardia Airport began to finger the night sky in the distance. Shortly they rolled up into the pool of dazzling lights that marked the entrance to the passenger depot.

Jerry said good-bye to his father in the car, a smile and a handshake. 'Good-bye, son. Take care of yourself.'

'Good-bye, sir.'

Looking at his father, sitting at the wheel of the roadster — pink-faced, fresh, young, looking smart as a clothing ad in tweed coat and bow tie — Jerry for a moment felt as though he were bidding good-bye to a stranger, someone who had picked him up and given him a lift. And then as he recoiled from the thought, his father's hand still holding his, he came to another, that it was himself at the wheel to whom he was saying farewell, perhaps forever. . . .

The hands of the clock over the information desk in the central waiting-room stood at one o'clock exactly as Jerry came in and found Eagles there waiting for him. The big pilot grinned appreciatively.

'Atta boy! I knew you'd be right on the button. My big shot arrived about ten minutes ago. We're taking off in half an hour. Well, how was it?'

Jerry had forgotten that he would have to report to Eagles, that his friend had ferried him across the ocean expressly so that he might see Catharine. He started to say: 'Gee, it was swell to be —' But luckily Eagles was occupied with thoughts of the coming flight as they made their way to the ATC Pilots' Ready Room.

Eagles said: 'I'll G-2 you on the way over. The weather looks okay. It'll be a breeze.'

A little later, Jerry sat strapped in his seat up in the big transport as it taxied down the field and parked off the runway while Eagles revved up his engines. Looking out of the window, Jerry could see in the distance the line of lights of the Queensboro Bridge and the dark outlines of tall buildings in the perpetual night glow of New York.

He was so exhausted that the sight meant nothing to him. He had never been quite so tired in all his life, not even after a hard mission. It was Sunday morning. He tried to think when he had last slept for a few hours. It was either Thursday or Friday. . . . When was it Patches had left for Kenwoulton? . . . It seemed ages ago. He could not focus his mind. The last thing he remembered was hearing, in Eagles's headset, the muffled voice from the control tower saying: 'ATC, C–87 at the east end of the field. You're cleared. Go ahead,' and the thunder of the engines beating the old takeoff tune. Lights began to slip past the window. . . . He was asleep before the wheels left the ground and tucked themselves into the belly of the silver ship.

Jerry slept all the way to Prestwick, where they came down through the overcast and landed in a drizzle. There Eagles passed him along to an RAF pilot who was ferrying a four-hundred-mile-an-hour Mosquito bomber to Basingwell Air-base, close to Kenwoulton. They took off at once, and fifty-five minutes later touched wheels to earth again. They transferred to a jeep and drove to town, where the pilot dropped him off with: 'All right if I leave you here, old man? I'm going on. You'll be able to find one of your chaps who'll give you a lift out to Gedsborough. Cheerio!'

It was shortly before nine o'clock Sunday evening that Jerry found himself standing outside the Crown and Arms at Wickle-gate Road in Kenwoulton in the blackout. It was still raining.

Jerry began to walk aimlessly through the rain and the dark-ness relieved only by the tiny red- and green-coloured crosses of the traffic lights, the faint gleam of the heavily shaded street lamps, and the ghost beams from the single low-voltage lights of the motor traffic. It smelled of summer rain and peat-coal smoke and beer. There was the noise of hundreds of feet shuf-fling on the pavement, and shadowy shapes of couples moved in a steady stream through the blackout.

He walked a little, then stopped and stood, and walked again like a man who is blind trying to find his way. The thickness of his long sleep had cleared from his brain, leaving in its place a growing confusion of thoughts and impressions, a kind of stag-gering bewilderment. Where was he? What world was this? Who and what were these shapes that suddenly peopled the darkness into which he had stepped only a moment ago from the brightness of his home on Long Island?

Surely if he could find the door through which he had just

come, he could step back into his father's panelled library. The scrabbling of Skipper's toenails on the hardwood floor lingered in his ears; he suddenly saw the moon face and pop eyes of Reston the butler with startling clarity, and heard the wheeze of the seltzer bottle as his father squirted soda from the siphon into a drink, the fat whining of the tyres of the roadster on the parkway. Manhattan lay just across the bridge. Turn another corner and he must see New York's glow and the Queensboro's chain of lights.

A couple brushed past him and he heard the man say: ' "And 'oo do yer think you are, just becos ye're a bloomin' sergeant major?" I says to 'im just loike that. . . .' An English voice; and all about him were English sounds and English smells and English stones beneath his feet, but they did not register with him.

He could not divorce himself from Westbury. The green and yellow bulbs of the Bijou Theatre sign ought to be blinking on and off and chasing one another around the rim of the marquee. Boys and girls in big, shiny roadsters or battered hand-painted jalopies should be driving by on a summer night's spin, laughing and kidding. And if physically he was in a British city, mentally he felt Westbury in him ten times more strongly.

His mind had failed to keep pace with his body, and the pictures that kept flashing across the screen of his consciousness were yet so recent that they appeared more alive and he lived them much more vividly than the strange shadowy moment of the present. They were all jumbled and mixed up in his mind – Catharine on the steps of the library in white skirt, light-blue jacket sweater, and blue bandeau around her head, his father proffering him the box of Havana cigars with the red-and-gold bands, the green bottle-glass of the Bailie Nichol Jarvie Bar at Aberfoyle, the feel of the turf beneath his knees when he knelt

178

and looked into Patches' eyes in front of Rob Roy's Cave, the white-and-purple Williams blanket folded at the foot of his bed, the smoky hotel in Glasgow. . . .

What had become of all the missing hours between home and Scotland and Kenwoulton? How much was true and how much a dream, which part was waking and which sleeping? Had he ever left Kenwoulton? Had he ever been home? Jerry remembered suddenly, with the sensation of approaching panic, how unreal he had felt in Westbury, the sense of being invisible and in a dream, and he struggled hard to keep a hold on himself.

But the struggle itself added to the fantastic sense of unreality, the loss of security, and the bewilderment in his mind. For now he found that he could no longer clearly remember or recapture anything – not Westbury, or Glasgow, or even Kenwoulton. He could not even believe the feel of the cobbles beneath his feet, the rain on his face, or the pungent odours of the English night. The panic against which he had been fighting fastened a firmer grip upon him, and he knew that he was losing his grip on himself.

Jerry felt as though he were suspended between heaven and earth in the grey overcast through which he had so often flown, that he was no more than a shadow adrift in a universe of shadows, and he felt too that he was dead and that the dead were walking beside him, two by two, boys and girls. He could hear, but he did not hear; he could see, but he did not see.

There was nothing left of the world he had known. Everything had retreated into the outer distances beyond regaining. He was lost and wandering adrift in a strange fringe of dark, swirling mists that would never lift.

He thought of Patches and of Catharine, of his mother and father and of his home, and they seemed many, many aeons of time and space away. He saw the earth as a whirling globe receding from him through the dark universe, growing smaller and smaller as it hurtled into eternity, and somewhere, infinitesimal upon its face, were all those he knew and loved. His mind turned to Gedsborough Airbase, the lumbering Liberators, and his companions: Sam Bognano, his pilot, Major Harrison, who had been his idol and his model, the men in his crew, who were dearer and closer to him than brothers. He was cut off from them all, perhaps forever. To find them again, to find anyone or anything he knew, would take many thousands of years of searching and wandering through strange and unfamiliar places. . . .

And in thinking of Patches, Jerry remembered a dream he had once and when he was a boy. It was of a brown-haired girl he had met upon a meadow, and they had loved each other. And then in the dream she had vanished and he had searched for her endlessly with an aching in his throat, a choking sadness, an unbearable desolation and loneliness in his heart for the beauty that had been, and he could never find her again. When he had awakened, nothing remained of the dream for a long time but the longing and the sadness.

And now it seemed as if he had recaptured this dream in all its poignant clarity, only it was a dream no longer, but reality. This was what had happened to him. He had shifted aspects, had turned like a looking-glass upon an axis and now faced the other way. All that had been reality – the war, his work, his friends, Patches and their honeymoon through Scotland, Main Street of Westbury with the jiggling marquee sign of the Bijou Theatre, the pop eyes of Reston as he let him into his home, home itself – took on the crazy, illogical, unrelated aspect of dreams. The dark fantasies that rose from the depths of his harassed and unhappy being had become reality.

The same choking sadness was in his throat, the same longing and desolation in his heart, but added were fear and the imminence of panic, and something even more terrible and desperate. He knew that he was in danger of breakdown.

It was no longer clear to him whether the enveloping night through which he moved, drained of everything but longing, sorrow, and despair, was the black of night or the darkness of the mind that might never lift.

With all his youthful health, vigour, and irrepressible vitality, not even the occasional attacks of nerves had been able to frighten him, but he was frightened now, for he felt himself no longer able to discern between reality and fantasy, and an abyss blacker than any night was opening up before him.

A dim light pierced the gloom through which he wandered, and instinctively, as does a moth, Jerry turned to it without knowing, and it drew his footsteps on. It came from a hanging street lamp, blacked out except for a small cone below that permitted one faint shaft to fall athwart the long, darker shape of human forms, ghosts like himself, huddling miserably in the rain in a queue along the edge of the pavement, waiting for a bus.

The bus queue in a blacked-out English town had become a part of Jerry's life since he had been based at Gedsborough, as were all the shapes and sounds of Kenwoulton at night, but he did not recognize them now. His mind did not react to familiar outlines and voices and smothered talk. Those, like himself, were the eternally lonely, the lost who peopled the darkness that lay beyond the universe.

But his gaze was caught upon the shaft of light descending perpendicularly from the small opening in the lamp above to where it fell directly upon a set, white face and illuminated it so that it alone stood out from all the darkness with a faint shining.

Jerry's eyes came to rest upon it, staring through the darkness, holding to the tiny spot of light in the gloom, clinging like a drowning man fighting for life, not daring to move lest it prove still another illusion of the dreams that tortured him, gazing, staring, trying to comprehend it with his mind, for it was the face of Patches. . . .

And as he gazed, still not daring to believe, he saw the shadowy outlines of her figure, wet, lumpy, the raindrops glistening from the heavy mackintosh drawn over her uniform and shining from the coils of damp hair beneath the military cap. It was safety, sanity, help and rescue, food and drink, journey's end, the sun, the moon, and the stars, and the joy of living – everything in nature, in heaven, and on earth that stirred the heart – it was Patches.

There it was, a white oval, the face of a plain, ordinary human being, marked with the curving lines of brows, the dark smudges of lashes, the ordinary familiar landmarks of the features – nose, mouth, and chin – and yet this one dear visage had the power, shining out of the black mists of the night that enveloped his spirit as well as his corporeal body, to halt the march of terror and panic that had laid hold of him, to dispel the dark, terrifying dreams, the confusion, and the aching loneliness.

Even greater was its power, for its presence, its shape and colour, its molecules, its being, were the miracle that cancelled the doom of the eternal and never-ending search upon which he had felt himself embarked. In the finding of it he had found himself with it. This face and person of Patches was not any imagining or dream. It was the beacon that beckoned him home after perilous flight – the friendly, comforting light shining in the darkness.

This was the stone in his heart, the pain in his throat, the longing and the loneliness. It was Patches. At last Jerry knew and understood the meaning of loving her, of knowing that nothing could ever wholly alter the need of her that had become a part of him, or the tenderness, warmth, and devotion that he felt for her.

For the first time he had a glimpse of understanding of the miracle of love and loving that transforms the commonplaces of flesh and blood into the lyric beauty of human relationship. She was music – was this girl – she was magic, she was goddess, mother, protectress, nymph, and witch, she was the earth and nature itself, with the power to restore him and keep him beyond all fear and harm. For even in the brief span of the instant in which he paused spellbound in the shadows by the glimpse of her, things that had so nearly slipped out of reach all about him became manifest again through his senses. Sight, sound, smell, and feel returned to him; he was aware again of the familiar shapes of houses in the blacked-out city, the touch of humans who brushed by him, the murmur of voices and muffled laughter, and the fresh, tangy scent of the rain mingled with the acrid, pressed-down coal smoke – the scent of England.

Because of the presence of Patches, the night and the rain and the grimy city became shot with swift and stabbing beauties that were all a part of the deep and boundless emotions moving him close to tears. He was like a wanderer who, returning after long years, yet hesitates and pauses on the threshold of the reality of all the yearning and nostalgic dreams, not for the moment daring to realize it because it had for so long been ardently yearned for and desired.

There was a heavy rumbling, and a dim, flickering eye pierced the darkness as the bus charged around the corner and screeched to a halt. The waiting line stirred and shifted, and in another instant the face of Patches would have vanished from the shaft of light, when Jerry sprang forward, shouting her name: 'Patches! Patches!' And as she turned at the familiar and so desperately longed-for sound of his voice, he reached her side and swept her into his arms, and held her there tightly, all wet and cold and shivery, as she had been once before, the night they were lost on the moors.

The bus conductor shouted: 'Come along now!' The line surged onward, pushing and scrambling to board the bus. No one looked, or stopped or bothered to notice the American flyer and the little WAAF with the white face who had been there a moment ago, for the darkness had swallowed them up.

They were together in each other's arms in a niche beneath a small stone gate-arch at the top of an alley, and Jerry held Patches close to him, saying: 'Patches ... Patches, I love you so. . . .'

He could not get enough of holding her so closely that he could feel her heart pounding deep beneath her clothes, of kissing her eyes, her mouth, her temples, even the damp cloth of her uniform because it was a part of her, of touching her face with his fingers, exploring her features, saying over and over that he loved her, as though in one torrential outburst he could make up to her all that he had once denied.

As though she had been lost to him for years instead of days he cried: 'Patches, I've found you. . . . I love you. . . . Will you marry me, Patches ... please, dear Patches?'

And Patches knew only that she was safe in Jerry's arms, sobbing: 'Oh, Jerry, don't let me go. Don't ever leave me again,' and that for the throbbing moment the darkness was lifted for her too. There had been no chance for her to think, to prepare herself. She did not know whence he had come or how he had found her, but only that she was in his arms, calling his name, answering his every desire for contact with her, giving him her mouth and her eyes wet with tears and rain, holding his face cupped in hands, straining her body to his so that it might never be torn away, making little sounds in her throat at each renewed touch of his lips or his hands, listening with her heart's blood to him saying that he loved her.

She was so parched and starved for the things he was telling her, the husky, broken sentences of love, that she was hearing him with her soul, soaking it up as a thirsty flower does the rain after a drought, and there in the darkness, clinging to him, her head pressed hard against his chest, as though she would lay her cheek against his heart, she began to live again, to swell with singing joy and happiness. The black abyss that had threatened to engulf her had closed; sweet earth upheld her feet again.

'Patches, I love you. . . .'

'I love you, Jerry. Forever. . . .'

'Will you marry me, Patches? You haven't said. . . .'

'Yes, Jerry. I will.'

'When?'

'Whenever –'

'Right away? Tomorrow? As soon as we can. . . .'

'Yes . . . I . . . Oh, Jerry, Jerry . . .' and the last was a different kind of a cry from her other calling of his name, and he felt her suddenly go limp in his arms.

For the mark of the hours she had spent since he had left her had cut deeply, the wounds were raw, and the memory of pain came through her happiness, and she did not think that she could bear to be hurt again.

Jerry said: 'Patches, darling, what is it? What's the matter?'

Patches was back in the officers' club at Gedsborough, across the table from Jerry, under the picture of the burning oil works, and she was hearing Jerry saying the words that had once come close to breaking her heart: 'I've got a girl back home. You know how it is. We're engaged. We're going to be married when I go back. . . .'

'Patches . . . what is it?'

She had to ask it. There was no escape. And though she might die from the doing of it, she had to remind him, to give him his chance, to make him think. She whispered: 'Jerry. . . . The girl back home? The one you were going home to marry? . . .'

In the time that elapsed between her question and Jerry's answer a thick drop of rain fell from the old stone arch above their heads and splashed on her brow, to run down her cheek and mingle with the tears.

'I'm not in love with her, Patches. I love you. There's no one but you. There never will be.'

But in that moment Jerry had travelled swiftly and far in his thoughts, faster than any ship of the air, faster than the speed of light. He had been to Westbury – his home, his room, Catharine's house, Main Street, and his boyhood – and back before he gave her his answer. And in the journeying a knowledge had come to him, and it was the knowledge of what it was to be a man.

There were many parts to this knowledge, some sweet, and some bitter, and in the clear vision that had come to him he seemed to see and understand each one and how they came to make the whole.

He knew for instance that he had never loved Catharine, because he had never understood the hunger, the pity, the power, and the terror of love. Nor might he ever have known but for the being called Patches and that which had come alive between them.

And it was another part too that there was once a boy, a

186

crazy kid, having himself a hell of a time flying an airplane with a bunch of good guys, a kid who wanted to grow up to be a man and who thought that to be a man he had to be like someone else, like Major Lester Harrison, for instance, gay and careless and free with women, reckless and hard and tough. And he had tried to be like him and found that that was not being a man at all. In the incalculably swift flash of his thoughts Jerry had even had time for a quick dart of pity for Major Harrison and to wonder what cross it was the major carried on his shoulders.

For you were a man only when you could be the things you were and face up to the truth without flinching or denying it. And the truth was that in life on earth there was no such thing as happiness without pain, victory without defeat. There were joy and enchantment and beauty to be garnered on the path, but at all times, too, there were burdens to be borne.

As to his own burdens, they were clear. They lay ahead of him. He would never wholly escape from them, never in the deepest sense be quite free of the guilt that would lie upon him from having brought hurt and pain to people who were dear to him.

But he had come to know the deepest implications of his relationship with Patches and what was meant by them. It was that, without her, life for him would be something but half lived, that to give her up would destroy not one, but two humans who together had found beauties and satisfactions of physical and spiritual relationship not dreamed of by most, and that to do so, to bring about that destruction, would be something evil and a sin.

And yet to take her, to yield to this need and love they had for each other, was no victory either, no certainty of happiness; and that, he knew also in this moment, was a part of being a man, that you could face up to your defeats and losses and reckon the price not too high to be borne for the sake of love.

Ahead of him yet lay the breaking of a human heart, with its inescapable burden of guilt and all of the distress he would bring to his family.

For when Patches had asked him the question about Catharine, Jerry had known that but for his knowledge that he loved Patches beyond all else, nothing had altered or come closer to solution. Everything was as it had been before when he had driven down to Prestwick, and must still be faced, but with one difference. He was a man and now had the strength to face it. He knew not only his mind, but his heart.

He could look ahead and see the trials and difficulties to come when he transplanted Patches from her background to his, the burdens that would be placed upon her, and the need there would be for love, understanding, and the insight and courage on his part to help her; he could catch glimpses of the obstacles that would be put in their way, and the scents of dangers and boredoms that would try them both when the adventure was over and romance turned into everyday living. She would always be an alien in an alien land with no one to turn to but him.

Nor could she help him with the guilt burden of the jilting of the girl to whom he had promised himself and whose life might be irretrievably wrecked by his decision. And this, too, Jerry was able to face as a man, for the war had taught him that life is pitiless and that there is forgiveness for many things, but not for weakness.

He had thought of his father and mother, of the kind of people they were, and it seemed as though for the first time he saw them clearly or understood them. For all of their years, they had never grown up as he had in a single night. Their life together – the life they had planned so carefully and lovingly for him – was adolescent and immature; and these things that had happened would wreck their plans; things over which they had no control would pain and confuse them immeasurably, particularly since it was he who had taken the ordering of his life out of their hands and into his.

But he knew too that they must bear this pain, even as he must be prepared to face what hurt or disappointment might lie before him because of what he was about to do, and he felt that in the end they would come to accept and even adjust themselves to it though things would never again be the same between them.

All in that final, infinitesimal splinter of time Jerry had felt upon his shoulders the weight of the burdens he would carry and the full extent of the price that would be exacted, and against the dear, fulfilling presence of this woman who had grown to be his, he knew that it was not too heavy for any man to bear.

'. . . there's no one but you, Patches. There never will be . . .'

His answer, the touch of his fingers on her face, holding it up to his, the deep tenderness of his kiss, satisfied Patches, re-awakened her heart, dispelling all clouds and hurts and fears, almost. She belonged to Jerry now, forever, and the singing within her was so loud and joyous that it all but quelled the little unease that was left.

They went away from the sheltered archway where they had been standing, hand in hand, holding hard to each other, not knowing quite where they were going, not caring. Another line was queueing up for another bus. And as they entered the little yellow circle of light from the blackout lamp above, the rays this time fell upon Jerry's face, and Patches, looking up as they passed, saw him for the first time.

And there was now no unease of any kind left within her, for it was another Jerry who walked beside her. Somewhere, somehow, he had left his boyhood behind him and had grown into a man. In his expression there were still the youth and gaiety and gentleness she loved, but behind it lay a strength and understanding that had not been there before. And seeing it, she knew that now, and for all time too, he belonged to her.